Joan's Summer

Heather Gardam

PROMONTORY
P R E S S

Promontory Press
www.promontorypress.com

ISBN 978-1-927559-86-4

Typeset by One Owl Creative in 14pt Minion Pro
Cover design by Marla Thompson of Edge of Water Design
Dad's drawings by Bill Gardam

Printed in Canada
0987654321

Dedicated to my husband Bill,
and our daughters,
Anne, Elaine and Gwyneth

Joan's Summer

Building

"Look, Joan!" exclaimed Patti as the kitchen door burst open. "Look at it now. Isn't it fantastic?" She glanced up as she tossed her brother Jamie's whittling knife onto the table and blew the sawdust off both ends of the peeled stick. Then she fitted it securely in place along the top of the log cabin wall, dovetailing each end into the side-pieces.

"It's going to be great, Joan. The best. And that's the last piece—now I'm ready for the roof." She beamed up at her friend—at the tall, thin figure, the dark untidy long hair, the frayed and faded jeans and t-shirt.

But Joan wasn't in an admiring mood. She was all hurried business, opening her pack. "Here, then," she said. "I copied some plans for the roof yesterday at recess."

She fished around in her jeans pocket and pulled out a much-folded piece of paper. "*And* I solved our problem," she added, turning to her pack and pulling out an old paper bag. "Look. The planks for the floor. The shakes for the roof. Remember?"

"What?" Patti didn't understand.

"My old popsicle sticks!" Joan announced as she tossed the rattling bag on the table and was already pulling a large book from her pack.

"Oh," said Patti, excited now. "Popsicle sticks—*perfect* boards! Nice and flat and easy to cut."

She jumped up and pulled out a chair for Joan.

Where did Joan get all her good ideas? On a day like this, Patti was so glad that she and Joan were working on this project together. Why, even the idea of a log cabin in a clearing, a model of a settler's homestead, had been Joan's idea. Patti was sure it was by far the most exciting project in the class. The other kids were making scrapbooks and posters showing how people made butter and cheese and soap and so on. Scrapbooks! Posters! She and Joan were making the *real* thing.

It was Saturday morning. The farm kitchen smelled of baking bread and Patti was in charge of watching it while Mom weeded in the garden. "Want some hot chocolate before we get started on the trees and stuff for the cabin yard?" she suggested.

"Nope," said Joan. She pointed at the book she had just dropped on the table. "I found that in the library too. Lots of pictures. Smokehouses. Bee-hives. Washing tubs and wringers. Lots and lots of things."

"Good ..." Puzzled, Patti watched Joan sling her pack back over her shoulder and head for the door. "Gotta run," she was saying. "Fast. Mom doesn't even know I'm here."

"But ... but I thought ..." Patti pointed at all the materials on the table. "We're doing the papier maché today, aren't we? You know—the cabin yard on this piece of plywood Dad found. Tree stumps and garden and stuff ..."

But Joan was already out the door.

"Joan—we've *got* to," Patti pleaded, following her to the doorstep. "It's got to be dry in time for us to paint it!"

"You go ahead," called Joan from the driveway. "See you in school on Monday."

Patti watched her duck through the trees into the shortcut through the garden. "There!" she exclaimed to nobody as she slammed the door. "That's *exactly* what you get when you try to do something with Joan!"

She looked at all her preparations on the table and she sighed. Joan was so much fun when she was with you—but in fact that didn't happen very often. She was brilliant at planning and finding books, but in the end, *who* read them, wrote out the notes, and then rewrote them after Joan had come up with her latest great ideas? Who actually *did* all the work?

I fall for it every time, thought Patti bitterly. What Joan needs is a full-time slave. She grabbed a sheet of newspaper and began to tear it into strips. She pulled one piece through the mixture of flour and water in the saucer, then began to wrap it around a fat stick to look like the stump of a felled tree.

Joan had been a frustrating friend ever since she moved to the small grey house at the crossroads right next to the gravel pit field. That was two years ago. Of course she knew Joan's family was a lot different from anyone else's around here. Joan was the oldest kid by far, and she had two small sisters and a brother. Patti didn't know anything about her father—she had never heard Joan mention him. They were poor, much poorer than Patti's own farm family. Patti could tell that because Joan never had any new clothes, even at Christmas, and she never had much in her lunch pail at school either. When her mom was sick—which was a lot of the time—it was Joan who had to look after everyone, even on school days. Sometimes it seemed to Patti that her friend was older than twelve. Sometimes she even seemed like the *real* mother in that family!

Patti sighed again. She supposed she understood why Joan had so little time to play or do school projects. But time was only part of the problem. There was Joan herself. Her attitude. Patti was her best friend at school, but that was only because she knew her best and could make allowances. And because most of the time she tried to ignore her cocksure, opinionated comments, the way she turned away from people when they were trying to be friendly. And the way she made promises she didn't keep. Like today.

Patti's hands had moved on from making tree stumps now, and were fashioning a vegetable garden: carrots, potatoes ... and what else? But her thoughts went back to Joan. The other kids had been friendly when she first arrived, she remembered. But after a while they just left her alone. Lately, they had started whispering about her— Patti had heard them. It made her sad and uncomfortable, but she guessed she didn't really blame them.

And that's my *real* problem, she thought angrily, standing up now to pull paper strips through the flour paste and lay them alongside the cabin walls to make the garden bigger. I understand *both* sides and sometimes I wish I didn't. I just don't *like* being caught in the middle. It doesn't fix anything, does it? It just makes me feel angry. And ... and helpless.

More newspaper strips needed. She stood up again to rip them, two at a time. *R-r-r-ip!* Three at a time! *R-r-r-ip!* That made her feel better. I wonder, she thought ... and this was an idea that had crossed her mind a few times lately: do I really *want* to be Joan's friend anymore? What if she makes me lose my other friends? What if they're whispering about *me* too?

Oh no! Patti jumped, scattering bits of paper as she darted to the oven. She pulled open the oven door and blew out a breath of relief as the hot, sour smell of baking bread enveloped her face. It wasn't burned, anyway—it was dark brown and crusty, but not burned.

"Is it okay?" asked Mom. Patti hadn't heard her come in. "I could smell it way out in the garden."

"Yep, it's okay," Patti answered as she put on the oven mitts and took the four loaves out, one at a time, and banged their sides hard on the work board to loosen them from their pans. Her face was red from more than just the hot oven.

"Did you forget it?" Mom was hanging her gardening sweater on a hook on the back of the door.

"Sorry, Mom. The timer must have gone off when I was outside saying goodbye to Joan."

"What happened with Joan?" Mom asked. "I thought she was going to work with you all afternoon."

"Gone home," said Patti, making a face. "As usual."

"Is her mom sick again?" Mom stood behind Patti to watch her begin poking toothpicks into the sodden newspaper garden to make a fence.

"I guess so. It looks like I'll have to do our project by myself. *Again*. It's due by the end of next week."

"Well …" said Mom, sitting down opposite Patti. "It certainly looks beautiful so far. I like that little tree you're making—an apple tree, I bet. It looks like fun. Do you think it would be okay with your teacher if your mother tore your newspaper into a few strips? Just for a few minutes?"

Patti grinned at her. "I won't tell," she said.

"You do understand about Joan, don't you?" Mom asked. "*Why* she doesn't stay and help you, I mean."

"I suppose so." Patti was struggling with her thoughts. "It's just … well, things are getting a lot worse lately."

"How so?"

"Joan's good at her school work, you know, and she likes it okay. But she misses *so* many days. And she's *always* late. She usually forgets her lunch. She wears her crummy old jeans and doesn't even brush her hair sometimes."

"How does Mrs. Thomas feel about all this, I wonder?" asked Mom as she got up to mix another bowl of flour and water.

Patti looked quickly up at her Mom. How did she know? "Well, that's the really weird part. Mrs. Thomas doesn't say anything about it at all. And that bugs all the other kids. I mean, what would happen to us if *we* did half of those things?"

"Yes," agreed Mom, "I can see their point of view."

"The other day," Patti went on, "Joan came in right in the middle of arithmetic. Almost lunch time, for crying out loud! She didn't even say she was sorry, just sort of swaggered in and sat down as if she owned the place. All

Mrs. Thomas said was 'Page forty-three' in a very quiet voice. Not mad at all!"

"Hmm," said Mom thoughtfully, staring out the kitchen window.

"Me too," said Patti, angry now. "I mean it makes me mad too. Well, embarrassed mostly, I guess. It even makes me wish she wasn't my friend!"

The model sat on the lawn in the Sunday morning sunshine, drying. The grass was high all around it, tops glowing a translucent green. Patti, on her stomach, with her head propped on her hands, was pretending that the roof was on already. She peered through the cabin's doorway, imagining it stood in the middle of a deep forest—in a clearing made by settlers a long, long time ago. Were there deer? Rabbits? What about skunks? Porcupines? Who would the people be, and why did they come here, anyway? Did they *like* it there in the woods—or were they scared?

A huge shadow moved silently over the cabin.

Rat-a-tat-tat!

"No, Chicky, no!"

Patti was on her feet just in time to stop a second *rat-*

a-tat-tat of Chicky's strong beak on the still soft papier maché.

She cradled her brown pet hen in her arms—the chicken that she had raised herself after it had survived a mink attack.

"Wouldn't you just *love* to eat my project," she exclaimed. "You … you Chicky monster!"

There was no sense in just taking Chicky around to the other side of the house—not now that she knew Patti was lolling about on the grass. There would be no getting rid of her! She put the chicken down and quickly picked up her model. Maybe the barn would be a safe place for it—there would be sunshine in the centre bay this time of day. High enough up to be out of reach, maybe on a stack of hay bales. Besides, she needed to borrow Dad's fret saw to cut the round ends off Joan's popsicle sticks. Today, while the paper dried, she must make the door-frame and the door of the cabin. Then she really should start work on the roof. It would be a long, picky job if she cut each shingle so that the roof looked like the picture in Joan's library book. How would she ever get it all done by Friday?

Dad was working in his workshop when she went to find the saw. "Why not use two pieces of plywood hinged together for the roof?" he suggested. "It would be so much faster. Then you can just paint them so they look like they have shingles on them."

"But they didn't *have* plywood in those days," objected Patti. "Did they?"

"No, you're right," laughed Dad. "But they didn't use popsicle sticks and papier maché to build their cabins either! It'll look just fine, don't you worry. I can cut the pieces right now, if you like." He reached for the plywood.

"The thing about the hinged roof," he explained, "is that you can lift the roof right off any time you like. You can work on the inside. Make a fireplace, maybe. Some furniture."

Patti looked at him with growing excitement. A fireplace! Furniture! If only she had more time! "Okay," she said. "Thanks, Dad. But you said hinges—what did they use for those? Not for the roof, of course, but what about the doors?"

"Well …" mused Dad as he reached down his saw from its pegs on the wall. "I'm pretty sure the settlers would have used leather for hinges if they didn't happen to have metal ones. And it probably worked quite well."

"Leather?"

"Yes—they made their leather from cowhide, and would always have had some on hand. Strong and flexible—it would have had many uses, and door hinges would have been one."

Dad carefully measured her cabin and cut the two pieces of plywood he had found in his scrap barrel. Then he handed her an old, folded piece of sandpaper and watched as she used it to smooth off the edges.

Jamie had come in while Dad was cutting the wood. He was getting so tall he had to stoop to peer through the door of the cabin, even though it was balanced up on three stacked bales of hay.

"Leather, eh," he said, "I wonder if we have any."

"Check Mom's rag-bag, Patti," suggested Dad. "Really heavy cloth would do too, for a model cabin. And think about gluing instead of nailing—the pieces will be so small."

"What I came to ask," said Jamie to Patti, "is if you want me to harness Little Guy to the wagon and give him some exercise. Since you're so busy."

Patti stopped sanding as she looked at him in alarm. She had completely forgotten about her little Quarterhorse, ever since she had fed and groomed him before breakfast and put him out in the pasture. Poor Little Guy! This was Sunday, his day for a special walk around the farm and some training with the wagon.

"Well?" Jamie was impatient.

But Patti still hesitated. She was glad, in a way, that Jamie had suddenly taken an interest in Little Guy last summer, once she started driving him in harness, but at the same time she didn't want her brother and her horse to spend *too* much time together. She didn't want either of them to forget whose horse he really was! On the other hand, she did need the time to work on the model …

"Thanks," she said at last, trying to sound pleased instead of grudging.

The sun had gone from the little cabin's perch in the barn. The roof was on now—the dim light disguising the fact that the plywood was still unpainted. Patti was trying to finish up her saucer of glue as she fashioned a chimney with small stones up the outside of the end cabin wall. She had almost reached the roof overhang, but the light was fading fast.

"So—how will you make the chimney go through the roof?"

Patti jumped, dropping the stone she had just covered with glue.

"I didn't hear you!" she exclaimed. "How did you get away from home, anyway—it must be nearly suppertime!"

"Stew's bubbling on the stove," answered Joan absently as she peered through the open door of the model cabin just as Jamie had done. "The kids are watching cartoons. Mom's asleep. I'll run back in a minute."

"Well ..." Patti was more than happy to explain, "you see, the roof comes right off! Dad's idea! The chimney goes up to the top of the wall—right there. Then ... see?

Dad's cut a wooden chimney that fits on top of the roof. I just have to cover it with stones. I can do that in the house tonight. Then we just have to be sure that the top chimney lines up with …"

Patti realized at last that Joan wasn't listening to her. Instead, she was gazing at the cabin as it sat in the deepening dusk, surrounded by its paper garden, unpainted trees, and a few hay spikes from the bale it was sitting on.

"It's *beautiful*," Joan said softly. "Just beautiful."

Patti watched, mouth open in amazement.

"Just think," Joan murmured, as if to herself, "a new place, a real little house. And it started from just an idea in our heads!"

"But it isn't *nearly* finished," objected Patti. "It'll look much better when it's painted. And later we can make furniture and stuff. Curtains. Whatever we have time for. Whatever *I* have time for," she corrected herself, with a sideways glance at Joan.

But Joan was deaf to sarcasm. She stepped over to the other side of the little cabin. "Imagine …" she said, "those people, those settlers, who left their homes, and look—now they have a home again. They dreamed it all up, and then they *did* it."

There was a long, awkward silence. Then Patti thought of something. "I could save the furniture and curtains for when you have time to do it with me," she offered. "Christmas, maybe? Easter holidays?"

Joan heard that. She turned to look at Patti for a long moment, her brown eyes thoughtful.

"Thanks," she said. Then she said it again. "Thanks."

Patti watched her slim, tall figure slip quickly out of the darkening barn.

Things Fall Apart

A shaft of early sunlight lit the log house and the clearing in the woods. Patti opened her eyes wider and stared at the finished project on her desk. The trees looked so *real* from the angle of her pillow, casting shadows over the pioneer garden and surrounding it in forest. Yet they were just popsicle sticks, tied into a teepee and covered with papier maché and painted—another one of Joan's ideas, muttered quickly to Patti the other day, as she dashed along the corridor and out the school door.

Joan.

Patti lay in bed for a few more minutes, just looking: a deep forest of pine trees, with paths winding mysteriously in and out—you could imagine getting lost in there.

Amazing. Then she thought about how confusing the past week had been, the whole project doomed one minute then fantastic the next. Would Joan help or wouldn't she? Would they finish on time? Would they still be friends when it was all over?

Patti sighed happily as she rolled out of bed. It was time to get it safely to school so Mrs. Thomas could finish her display for the year's big parent-teacher night—"The History of Our Farms". Would Joan be at school to see it once it was up? Well, it didn't matter. Today, anyway, everything seemed worth the hassle to Patti and nothing was going to bother her. She was staring at the chimney now, noticing how the tiny rocks seemed like big ones on that little cabin. It was all magic, really, making things like this. But then her projects always seemed that way to her—a bunch of ideas, and lots of worry and work and then more ideas and more work, and bingo! Suddenly something was there that hadn't been before! Patti was pulling on her t-shirt when she thought of something else: this cabin in the woods wasn't just a *thing* they had made; it was a different *time* too. A long-ago time. This was definitely magic.

A door banged downstairs. Patti glanced quickly at the little red alarm clock on her desk. She reached for her barn jeans, because she still had her outside chores to do, then she flipped the covers back over the bed to tidy it, and headed for the stairs. Today she had to be ready twenty minutes earlier than usual, because Dad had promised to pick up Joan and take them both and their model to school on his way to the mill. And she had promised to phone Joan early to be sure she was ready—they couldn't risk making Dad late for work.

"What about phoning Joan before chores?" Mom suggested.

"Yeah," Patti agreed. "No excuses today!"

But for a long time there was no answer to the ringing, ringing, ringing. Were they all still asleep?

"Oh no," muttered Patti. "Come *on*, Joan! Don't be asleep."

Click. The receiver was lifted at the other end. "Hi, Joan? Joan?"

But there was no answer. Was it one of the little kids? Why didn't they *say* something?

"Hello? Hello?"

Mom peered into the dark hallway, eyebrows raised in question. Patti shrugged back at her and shook her head.

And then, at last, there *was* a voice—a strange, muffled voice. "Joan? Is that you?"

Suddenly Mom was beside Patti. She took the phone. "Joan? This is Helen. Is something the matter?"

Something *was* the matter, Patti was sure.

Mom listened for a minute or so. Then she spoke carefully and slowly. "Joan," she said, "I want you to sit the children up to the table for breakfast. Get them out of bed and settled in the kitchen. Do you have some cereal? Good. Milk? Can you do that? I'll be there in just a few minutes. Are you okay with all that? Good girl."

"What is it?" asked Patti.

But Mom didn't answer except to shake her head. White-faced, hands shaking, she dialled two of the emergency numbers on the wall beside the phone: police and ambulance. And now Dad was in the hall too. And Jamie. Patti hadn't heard them come in from the barn.

"Something has happened to Joan's mother," Mom said at last, when she had hung up the phone. Her voice was shaky, like her hands. "I'll have to miss work, Bob. Joan needs me there … there's so much … all those kids …"

"You go ahead, honey," Dad said, his voice deep and calm through the fog that seemed to envelope Patti there in the hallway. "We can look after things here. I'll phone the bank to tell them you won't be there. And I'll go in to the mill later on—it won't hurt to be a bit late today, so I can come and help you soon. In half an hour or so. Okay?"

Now Mom was reaching behind the kitchen door for her gardening sweater, then stopping in the open doorway.

"Kids, you'll have to make your lunches yourselves. And finish your chores quickly, you don't have much time before the bus."

She grabbed her purse, ready to go. And then she was just standing there, looking at them for a long moment. She didn't look like Mom, thought Patti, suddenly afraid. Finally, she was gone.

It wasn't till later, sitting at her desk in school, that Patti realized she had completely forgotten about her model cabin. She and Jamie could maybe have managed it together on the bus if they had thought of it. But really, it didn't seem to matter much anymore.

All day she was aware of Joan's empty desk near the front of the room. And every time she left the room, she looked at the bulletin board at the back, covered with all the bright posters that had been handed in on time. And the display table where Mrs. Thomas had left a large space for the cabin. It hadn't even come yet, Patti thought every time she walked past—so why did it look as if it had been taken away?

Tonight, Patti didn't want to go up to her room. It was getting late, she knew: Mom had already looked up from her sock mending with a question in her eyes. Until a few days ago, Patti had always preferred reading in bed in the evening, rather than in the living room. Snuggled in cozily, she usually dropped off to sleep early, especially in summer when wake-up time was sunrise.

But now ... now her room was no longer *her* room. It wasn't inviting anymore. Patti wasn't sure when exactly the change had happened. It was she, after all, who had offered to share her room and everything in it, eager to think up ways to help in Joan's emergency after her mother died of heart failure.

So Joan's narrow bed had come from her house and been placed along the opposite wall from Patti's bed, where her dresser used to be. The dresser and the bookcase had been squashed together beside the door. There was still room for Patti's desk under the window between the beds, but it was a shared desk now, with a reading lamp on both sides. The globe Uncle Henry had given Patti for Christmas had been sent downstairs to its new place on top of the piano. Patti's good dresses and blouses had ended up in Mom and Dad's closet to make room for Joan's few hanging clothes and a box of bedding from Joan's house on the closet floor. Even the dresser was shared—Patti had found two cardboard boxes for her pants and sweaters and pushed them under her bed.

"I don't need those drawers," Joan had tried to insist, in that dull, stubborn voice she used these days. "I don't have that many clothes."

"For your special things, then," Patti had said.

Two of the dresser drawers now held a collection from

the grey, wooden house at the crossroads on the way to town: the calendar of the Grand Canyon from the kitchen wall; two glass vases; a portable radio; an old, crocheted, beige-coloured shawl that her mother had worn; two battered photograph albums and a few scrapbooks; Joan's old report cards and a bundle of Christmas and birthday cards. A framed photograph of Joan's parents on their wedding day—a black-haired, slim, smiling young woman and a tall, dark-skinned young man squinting into the sun.

"Don't you want this up on the dresser?" Mom had asked as she helped Joan unpack her boxes.

But Joan shook her head silently and put it away in the bottom drawer.

Joan had seldom been in Patti's room in the years before her mother died. Their friendship had been mostly an outdoor one. But now, in a week, she and her possessions had taken over the room. At least, that's the way it seemed to Patti. Joan stopped making her bed in the mornings after the first two days, and her clothes, shoes, and school books lay scattered on the floor most of the time. This was a surprise to Patti—wasn't it Joan who had tidied, cooked, and washed dishes to keep her family reasonably organized? Had she changed?

But it wasn't really the messy room that upset Patti; it bothered her that it *bothered* her. She used to leave her room pretty messy herself, didn't she? When she was busy with other things? So … why did it matter?

But it did. And she was too ashamed to even mention it to Mom. Especially since both Mom and Dad spent so much time and effort making things easier for Joan while she was staying at the farm. Jamie too. *They* didn't notice Joan's untidiness, or the fact that she hardly ever said anything—not even "thank you". She didn't help with anything anymore.

"Wouldn't Joan be happier with her *own* family?" Patti asked now, tentatively, closing her book and watching Mom with her needle and wool. Joan was up in bed, reading her way through Patti's collection of *Nancy Drew* books, and Dad and Jamie were in the kitchen, planning a woodworking project for the summer holidays, which were only three days away. Mom and Patti were alone in the living room.

Mom didn't look up from her work. "Joan's Aunt Kate talked that over with us," she reminded Patti gently. "She *does* want Joan to live with her eventually—Aunt Kate is Joan's dad's sister, you know, and she and Joan have always been special friends. But her place is too crowded with the three little kids to take Joan right now. You see, even if things work out the way she hopes they will, her brother can't drive out from Calgary to get the little ones until the end of the summer."

Patti sighed. She knew all that already.

Mom looked up. She smiled at Patti in a way that

seemed to understand how she was feeling.

"There's more to it than that, though," she said. "I think it might help you if I told you about it. But I don't want you to discuss it with Joan. Okay?"

Patti sat up. She nodded.

"You know how you've always complained that Joan had so little time to play? Well, Aunt Kate has been worried too. She wants to keep her niece here for as long as arrangements are up in the air—away from the relatives and the negotiations—because she's afraid that Joan will end up, once more, the main person looking after the kids. She has always done it, after all, and she's good at it. I bet she even misses it right now."

"Really?" said Patti. She hadn't thought of that.

"I'm sure she does. But that feeling won't help her situation, Aunt Kate thinks. To the grown-ups, it's bound to seem an easy solution to a difficult problem—even to Joan herself. But Aunt Kate is determined to keep Joan with her and give her some time to be a child herself—to make friends, take some music lessons, and have time for her schoolwork. And your Dad and I agree with her."

This was interesting—Patti was feeling better already. "I agree, too," she said.

Mom smiled again and went back to her stitching.

"It's lucky Aunt Kate's a teacher and can afford all those telephone calls from the city," Patti observed, drily.

Mom laughed and nodded.

Talking on the phone to her family was the only time Joan *did* talk, Patti thought, but she decided not to say it out loud. Joan had insisted on going back to school the day after the funeral—after Aunt Kate, who had brought the little ones back from the city for the day, had kissed Joan good-bye and promised to phone every evening after supper so she could say good night to the kids. For half an hour Joan chattered away to each one in turn, cheerful, encouraging, even laughing sometimes.

The rest of the time she had nothing to say.

Things were even worse at school. Everyone just assumed that Patti would stay with Joan and "look after" her. They were sympathetic now, kinder than they had been before. But that didn't mean their recess and lunchtime play would change. Patti watched from the school steps as the others raced toward the softball diamond— first there, first up to bat—laughing and calling to one another. She tried to ignore them by "helping" Joan with homework she should have done the night before instead of reading late, with her light shining in the bedroom long after Patti had fallen asleep with the covers over her head.

But Joan didn't really need help. Today, for instance, they had drilled each other for the big, end-of-year spelling bee, and then Joan had won as usual. But all the time she had that new blank and uncaring sort of expression that Patti hated. It put so much distance between her and the other kids, and it made Patti feel alone.

Patti watched Mom now as she threaded her needle with red yarn and reached for a red sock. It was Joan's sock. Frustration came rushing back. If only school could be the way it used to be! If only her family was *hers* again! And her room.

"How *long* does she have to stay?" The question burst out of its own accord, harsh and resentful. Patti was appalled.

But Mom didn't seem surprised at all. "I know this isn't easy for you," she said, quietly, without looking up. "But you know, Patti, we're only doing for Joan what I would hope and trust that someone would do for you and Jamie. If the same thing ever happened in *our* family."

Patti stared at Mom, shocked. Did she really think such a thing could happen to *us*?

Fences

Patti ran all the way from the barn to the house. The June morning air was cool and fresh, and today was the last day of school! If I don't miss the bus, she thought suddenly. She glanced at her watch as she reached the back screen door.

"You should have been up earlier, Patti," said Mom sharply. She was finishing the lunches, folding down the tops of the row of brown paper bags.

Patti looked at her, surprised. Mom didn't often sound so cranky. "Well, you've almost missed the bus three days in a row, haven't you? Maybe you need to do your barn chores faster or something. You *know* I can't take time out to drive you, or I won't get *my* chores done!"

Patti shrugged helplessly. She looked at Joan, still eating cereal at the table, unaware, staring off into space.

"Hurry *up*, Patti!"

Her mouth set in an angry line, Patti took the stairs two at a time. Joan had been almost impossible to wake up that morning, and when she finally did get up and go into the bathroom, Jamie was already back from the milking, expecting to get *his* shower.

"What am I supposed to do now?" he had hissed furiously at Patti. As if it were *her* fault.

And now, as Patti dashed to the bathroom to wash her horsey-smelling hands and brush her teeth, she realized that Jamie was still in there with the door shut. "I'll just have to do without," she muttered. Slipping out of her barn clothes, she tossed them angrily on the floor beside Joan's. She grabbed clean pants, pulled out a sweater box from under the bed because it was still cool in the classroom sometimes, then stuffed her school books into her book bag. As she was heading for the door, she remembered Joan: back she went to find a sweater for her. Where? Ah, there on the bed. School books? Already packed, thank goodness.

In the kitchen, Mom was talking to Joan. "No thanks," she was saying patiently. "You can help with the dishes tonight, if you like. It's time to run for the bus now."

As if she doesn't *know* that, thought Patti furiously, her running shoes crunching the gravel behind Jamie and

Joan's longer legs. She's been with us nearly two weeks already. She knows the routine perfectly well. *She* goofs around, spoils everything, and then everyone blames *me*!

It was during the short bus ride, her face up against the window to watch the early summer morning speed by—the fields, the gravel pit, the closed-up house at the crossroads, the next farm—it was then that Patti made her decision. Today was her last chance to play a game with her classmates before summer holidays. She would let Joan sit on the school steps by herself, if that's what she wanted to do. But Patti would spend the half hour before the bell doing what *she* wanted to do for a change.

It seemed such a long time since she had played with her friends. There were those terrible days right after Joan's mother died, of course. At first she hadn't even felt like playing, and after that she knew she should stay with Joan. But even before that … Patti watched the first houses of the town sweep by as she remembered the two weeks of busy work on the log cabin project, looking up books in the library, writing up the building process, planning with Joan.

The log cabin. What a long time ago that seemed— yet it had only been a few weeks. An altogether different life—a much *better* life, too. The model was in the glass display case in the front entrance hall of the school now. How beautiful it looked with its garden and surrounding forest. And it would still be there, Mrs. Thomas had promised, when they came back to school in the fall. Patti felt better whenever she thought about the log cabin—that, at least, had turned out well. She wondered if she and Joan would make the furniture and stuff in the summer as they had planned. She wondered if she and Joan would ever do *anything* together again.

The bus was bumping along the school driveway, pulling up now by the white fence. Patti was first off the bus. She ran up the path to drop her sweater and book bag on the school steps. Good—a couple of her friends were already on the softball diamond. That meant they had already fetched the ball, bat, and gloves from the janitor, beating the older kids to it—they would have to play soccer instead of softball now, something that didn't happen often.

She stopped for a moment, seeing Joan behind her. "I'm going to play ball now," she said.

Did Joan even hear? She already had the *Nancy Drew* book out of her bag and was sitting down on the steps.

Racing out to the field, behind the others now, Patti felt a little shy—like a stranger in her own school.

"Hi!" called Sylvia from her place at the pitcher's mound. "Only outfield left, I'm afraid!" But Patti could tell she was pleased to have her back in the game.

Outfield's just fine today, she decided, though this was something that would have discouraged her before. There was heaps of time for her to work her way up to bat and, anyway, the sun was shining warmly and the playing field smelled of freshly cut grass.

She ran to the trouble spot, well behind the second and third bases—this was the "outfield" for her school. It was right in front of a high wooden fence belonging to the house next door. Whenever the ball soared over that fence, the fielder had to run all the way to the roadside opening of the school fence, then frantically search the bushy garden for the ball. It was a "for sure" home run, which meant the hitter stayed up to bat even longer. It also took up a lot of their precious playing time, as everyone else stood around and waited. Better by far to stop the ball before it went over there. Patti jogged on the spot for a few minutes as she watched the play—she wanted to be ready for a sprint.

"Hi Patti!" Ruth was waving a welcome from her place at shortstop. Patti grinned happily. It was good to be back!

It was a strange game, though. Patti was soon puzzled: where was the usual hard-hitting zest? Though Patti was ready for them, there were no "fence balls" at all—only dribbles, an unusual number of foul balls and more strikeouts than Patti could ever remember. Even Susan, a tall, athletic redhead, and an almost certain home-run hitter, sent a ball zooming along the ground straight to first base and put herself out. What was going on? Patti shook her head in amazement as she ran from one position to the next in rapid succession.

At last Patti stood in front of the pitcher, giving the bat a few practice swings. Well, here goes, she thought. She took a deep breath and watched Susan closely—she was a tricky pitcher sometimes. She felt all the frustrations of the past weeks spend themselves in that one, glorious, satisfying *crack!* of the ball against the bat. Joyfully, she dropped the bat and began to run.

The others stood, watching the ball soar, eyes shielded from the sun. But there was none of the usual yelling, the shrieked advice to the fielder. No teasing comments as she flew past first base, second base. Hey! There was no one *at* second base! Patti stopped to look around. The whole game was dissolving; people were picking up their books and jackets, heading back to school in groups. There were glum expressions everywhere. No one looked at Patti.

"What's going on?" Patti asked Sylvia who was coming in from outfield. "The bell didn't go already, did it?"

"What do you mean, what's going on?" snapped Sylvia. "You hit the ball over the fence, *that's* what's going on!"

"But … but …" Patti looked at her friend, completely puzzled.

"You *must* know about the fence," Sylvia said. "I mean, how could you miss it? For days we've been trying to hit that stupid ball so it wouldn't go over that stupid old fence!"

"But why *not*?" asked Patti, mystified.

Sylvia looked at her strangely for a minute. "I suppose

you've been away for awhile … sort of," she said at last. She began to walk toward the school and Patti fell into step beside her.

"There are new people in that next-door house now," Sylvia explained, "and the man's been complaining to the principal about the ball in his garden. Especially about us going over there to look for it. So now there's a new rule: if the ball goes over, we have to quit the game until the secretary can phone the guy who lives there and get his permission for one of us to go and look for it. And we can only do that *after* school."

The two girls walked the rest of the way in gloomy silence.

There was an end-of-school assembly first thing that morning, put on by the grade eights. Back in the class-room, Mrs. Thomas had jobs for everyone, sorting and tidying, emptying the desks, accounting for all the text-books and carting them off to the storeroom. When even the bulletin boards had been dismantled and the waste-paper baskets emptied, it was time for report cards. Then Mrs. Thomas gave a nice speech about what a pleasure it had been to have them in her class and how she looked forward to seeing them again in the halls in September. All this had been done in the midst of such a cheerful, comradely buzz that Patti hoped against hope that the others had already forgotten her terrible goof that morning.

But Patti hadn't forgotten. She was quiet and kept as busy as she could while the others joked and teased all around her. When Ruth suggested she come to spend a day on her farm the next weekend, she accepted the invitation awkwardly, her smile pasted on her face. It was the same later, when Sylvia yelled, as she was disappearing onto the other bus, "See you at Carolyn's stables tomorrow, Patti! It's summer! Yay!"

Since it was only a half-day at school, Mom had left their lunch bags for them in the kitchen. Patti took hers upstairs with her to change into her riding clothes. As she came slowly down the stairs, she listened for Jamie and Joan; they were still there, in the kitchen, talking quietly. The fridge door slammed. She remembered that Jamie would soon be hurrying off to help Maynard for the afternoon with some fencing—now that he was fourteen, Dad was hiring him to work on the farm half a day during the summer. That meant that Joan would be alone ...

Too bad, thought Patti. She needed, really *needed*, to spend the afternoon with Little Guy, getting ready for her riding lesson tomorrow. Maybe, if she worked really hard, maybe if she just had a chance to be alone for a while, she would feel better. Get her life back to where it used to be before … well, before Joan came to live with them.

Patti looked at the rarely used front door. She could still hear noises in the kitchen. Quietly she turned the key that was always in the lock, and let herself out; in her socks she crept along the grass that bordered the side of the house, ducked as she passed the main kitchen window, then eased open the screen door to the back kitchen. She reached around to get her riding boots and hat. Finally she was off to the barn. She was free. Soon she would forget all the things that had gone wrong lately.

If only Jamie had forgotten.

Patti, tired and sore from a long afternoon's workout, was washing up in the upstairs bathroom before supper. She definitely felt better, she decided. She could hear Mom shifting pots around, opening and shutting the oven door. It was time for her to get down there and get that table set.

Jamie's head appeared around the open bathroom door.

"Nice going today, Pats," he said in his usual teasing voice. "What were you trying to be? The champion batter of the world?"

Suddenly all Patti's anger came flooding back. Guilt, too—she still didn't know what Joan had done with her afternoon alone. "I didn't *know* about the fence rule!" she shouted at Jamie. "How *could* I know? *You* sure didn't tell me!"

Jamie pulled back, surprised. "But *everyone* knew about it."

"Well *I* didn't! How could I? I never get a chance to play with the kids anymore. Nobody tells me what's going on! And everyone blames me for everything! And it's all because of Joan! Because she's living here!" Patti was crying now.

Jamie was shocked. "Where *is* she, Patti?" He whispered. "Where's Joan?"

Patti shook her head, wiping her tears on a towel. "Downstairs, I suppose," she muttered. "With Mom. In the kitchen."

But she wasn't. Jamie tiptoed down the stairs to check, then along the upstairs hall to peer into the bedrooms. He reported to Patti that Joan was on her bed reading, with the door open. She must have heard every word.

Patti washed her face again to get rid of tear tracks, then hurried downstairs to help Mom. She knew she should go and apologize to Joan right away, but what if Mom heard? The best thing would be to do it later, when they were alone in the bedroom with the door shut.

It was a long and awkward dinner for Patti. In spite of all her exercise that afternoon, she wasn't hungry. Joan was quiet, as usual, and Patti had nothing to say either. It was Jamie who kept Mom and Dad entertained, telling them about his work with Maynard. Then he told them about a friend at school, and then all his summer plans.

Every now and then he looked anxiously at the two girls. Did her parents know that something was wrong? Patti hoped not. She hoped that it would all be sorted out soon, before they had a chance to find out.

After supper, Joan helped Patti dry the dishes and it was Mom who chattered while Jamie and Dad spread plans out on the table again. Then Joan disappeared upstairs to read, and Patti tried hard to concentrate on a game of checkers with Mom.

"That was much too easy," Mom announced, clearing off the last of Patti's men. "What's up?" she said, looking at Patti suspiciously.

"I guess I'm just tired," said Patti.

Slowly she made her way up the stairs, trying to think of the right way to say she was sorry. But she needn't have worried; Joan's light was out already, and the figure under the covers was still.

Patti wished *she* could sleep. How could a person be so tired and still not be able to sleep? She tossed and turned long after Mom and Dad had put out the hall light.

Running Away

Riding lessons. Patti was so glad it was summer at last and she was on her way back to riding lessons this cool, clear, sweet-smelling morning. She stood on her bike pedals to puff up the last hill before she reached Carolyn's stables. Her mind was busy too, planning her morning.

Stable work first, of course, because that's how she and her friends, Eric, Jenny, and Mary, earned their lessons with Carolyn. She hadn't seen the other three since the Fall Fair last September—they lived in a neighbouring town and went to a different school. But they were coming back. Thank goodness for that, she thought, walking her bike alongside the quiet paddock and leaning it up against the toolshed: working together made fun out of grooming horses and cleaning out stalls. Racing each other, they would soon get their morning chores up to last summer's speed.

Was she the only one here so far? Patti peeked into one stall and then the next, then she ran to find a hoof pick and brushes. She would start the summer right by finishing first. Luckily, she got to choose which end of the stables to start on.

"Hi, Muffin," she said to the old grey horse at the far end. "You get to be first!"

A soft nose nuzzled her hand. "Six horses to do. That should take about two hours. Then we get to ride for an hour. I'll be on one of Carolyn's horses this year—but not you, old thing." She stopped to give the nuzzling head a good rub around the ears.

Patti wasn't a mere beginner anymore. What's more, she and Little Guy had surprised everyone by coming first in the flat class in the Fall Fair show last year, beating all the fancy horses and ponies and more experienced riders. Of course, it was mostly Little Guy who was responsible for that, but still, it had done wonders to improve her lowly beginner status. And Little Guy was no longer a lame horse, but a hero!

And now there was this new arrangement that Carolyn had discussed with Dad on the phone: either Dad or Maynard, their hired farm hand, would trailer Little Guy to the stables every second Saturday so that

Mr. Anderson could use him to teach some of Carolyn's students how to drive a horse pulling a wagon. Driving-in-harness it was called.

Mr. Anderson, whose family owned Little Guy, had taught Patti and her horse to do this last summer—it was something to occupy them both while Little Guy was still healing from the big splinter that had been pulled from his foot. For a sad while it had seemed that Patti might never be able to ride the little horse that she had nursed back to health. But these days he was all better, except that he would probably never be able to go back to show jumping. That didn't seem to matter to Patti anymore, though, now that he was definitely hers to look after and ride for as long as they both wanted to. However, Mr. Anderson and Carolyn had persuaded her that it would be a good thing for Little Guy to be used to interest other kids in driving-in-harness.

"We don't want to keep all the fun under our hats, do we?" Mr. Anderson had said cheerfully. "Little Guy's at his best, anyway, when he's teaching someone. *You* should know that!"

Yes, thought Patti, smiling to herself as she pitched fresh sawdust into a stall and remembered her struggles with Little Guy last summer, until she finally understood that he was the one who knew best. Mr. Anderson was right.

There was so much to look forward to. As Patti

brushed a big bay Thoroughbred, she sighed her gratitude that this was so. She was especially glad that every morning of the week, except Saturday and Sunday, she would have to be here and away from the farm, busy with something that demanded her whole attention. There would be no time to worry about Joan.

Was that Joan again, creeping into her thoughts? Darn!

Joan had been out of bed already when Patti's alarm clock went off that morning. There was no sign of her in the house, and none in Little Guy's summer paddock when she gave him his grain and water and a big hug around his shaggy neck. Was she somewhere in the barn where Dad and Jamie were doing the milking? Or maybe in the garden with Mom?

In any case, Patti had been in a hurry—there was simply no time to look for Joan or talk to her. That apology she had rehearsed over and over again in the dark last night would just have to wait. Patti didn't know whether to be happy about that, or sorry she couldn't just get it over with.

If only … well, if only she had just gone and said she was sorry right away—right after she had said that terrible thing. She had been so angry about everything, at school and at home. But that wasn't really Joan's fault, was it? How could Joan help feeling sad because her mother had died and her brother and sisters were far away in the city? And then Patti had just piled more trouble onto her friend. She had blamed Joan for her *own* feelings!

Patti had suspected that Joan might have gone back to her old house early that morning, the first day of the summer holidays. But when she passed by on her bicycle half an hour ago, she was surprised to see that the door was not open nor were the blinds raised. After all, Joan had been going there every now and then to get something she had forgotten, or just to check that her old home was still the way she had left it. Dad had arranged a hiding place for the key, and told Joan that she could go there whenever she liked until the end of the month. At that point, he and Mom would help her clear out whatever was left, and hand the house over to the landlord.

But today the house had been quiet, its windows as blank as if it, too, had died on that strange morning three weeks ago. Patti slowed her bicycle as she scanned the yard, the front door, the back porch, on her way past this morning. She had sighed with relief. And that was when she started to wonder about herself: wouldn't it have been a *good* thing to find Joan and get the apology over with? Surely that would have made them both feel better … yet she had been *glad* not to see Joan at the house. What kind of person was she, anyway?

Patti stopped her brushing for a moment to lean out the stall window. Ah, there they were at last—all three of the other stable workers, rattling their bikes down the lane toward her.

Good, she thought, tossing her brush down and heading out to meet them. People to talk to! Then a hard riding lesson still to come—something to focus on and learn to be good at. She badly needed this holiday from Joan. Maybe, sometimes, it's not a bad thing to run away from your problems!

"Is that you, Patti?" Mom was calling from upstairs. "Hi!" Patti yelled back cheerfully. It had been a good morning after all. But she was tired—oh, how her arms ached from the unaccustomed shovelling of so much sawdust, and the way Carolyn's horse pulled on the reins. She would have a whole new set of problems to learn about with that Berry, a chestnut mare who clearly liked to be the boss whenever she could get away with it. Patti could hear Mom running down the stairs. Patti gulped a glass of water, ready to tell her all about the morning.

"Have you seen Joan?" Mom's usually sunny face was drawn with anxiety.

"No. She was already gone when I woke up this morning. Isn't she back yet then?"

"There's no sign of her." Mom rubbed her forehead.

"Your Dad and I are getting worried, Patti. There are some things missing from your bedroom, you see—her school pack, and both her heavy sweaters and her extra jeans. And her pyjamas."

Mom went to the stove to pour herself some coffee. When she turned to lean against the stove, the look she gave Patti was a searching one. "I understand she overheard you saying some rather resentful things last night?"

Patti could feel her face redden. She nodded, looking at the linoleum. Then she felt the stirring of anger. "Jamie told you, didn't he?"

"Only when we started to get really worried." Mom was sipping her coffee and looking at Patti with that considering expression.

"I'm sorry," Patti said, the anger suddenly gone again. "I didn't *mean* to … it just sort of … I thought she was downstairs somewhere. I wish I hadn't said it. I was planning to apologize this morning, but she was gone."

Mom nodded. "This has been a difficult time for us all," she said gently. "Getting used to having a new member of the family. A badly *hurting* new member at that." She was quiet for a few moments, thinking. "If Joan were to run away, where do you think she would most likely go?"

Run away? Patti's head was in a whirl. Had she made Joan feel *that* bad?

"Dad has checked her house already," Mom went on.

"He looked around and decided she has probably taken some pots and pans and cutlery—cooking stuff. There were cupboards and drawers left open in the kitchen. Also, there seem to be some old blankets missing from the kids' beds."

Would Joan really run away?

"I checked our pantry too," Mom was saying. "There's a loaf of bread missing. Some eggs gone from the bucket in the summer kitchen, I'm pretty sure … I would guess she's thinking about camping …"

Patti interrupted. "Should I run down and see if she's gone to our playhouse?"

"Good idea," agreed Mom. "I think we should check everywhere we can think of first. Dad and I decided to wait the morning out to give her some time alone, if that's what she needs. But now it's time to start doing something. We think the weather looks good, at least for today, so we don't want to phone Aunt Kate or the police until it gets closer to dark."

The police!

That thought sped Patti down the familiar path, past the orchard, the beehives, over the foot bridge, and into the woods. Her aches and pains from her morning's efforts were forgotten.

But the little shelter was empty. "Joan!" called Patti. "Joan!"

Silly, she told herself; if Joan really ran away, why

would she come out of hiding just because Patti called? Especially Patti—the one who made her so unhappy in the first place.

And there was something else: Joan was absolutely the best person in the world at hiding in the woods. Patti was remembering a day last summer, down in the big woodlot across the road—how Joan had dodged behind bushes and trees, playing the spy. She had climbed high among leafy branches and crouched behind old stumps, always managing to stay hidden while Patti and Little Guy worked with Maynard to haul felled trees out of the underbrush.

"She's good," Maynard had observed then. "*Real* good."

Patti guessed that if Joan didn't want to be found, she probably wouldn't be.

Pushing open the barnyard gate, Patti thought again about that woodlot at the bottom of the big hayfield across the road. Wouldn't that be a good place to look? There might be at least some traces of Joan if she was there—she had to leave all those things she carried *somewhere*, didn't she? Even if she stayed hidden herself.

Patti began to run back to the house. This time, she would take Little Guy to help.

Mom had insisted on lunch and a planning session before they all set off again on their different assignments, so it was almost an hour later that Patti turned Little Guy down the wagon track toward the woodlot. By the time she was over the crest of the hill in the big field, she could hear Dad's pickup zoom out the driveway, then on to the main road. He had Jamie with him.

Dad's plan was to go and talk to a few of his friends in town and on farms close in, so that their sharp eyes could be on the lookout even before they had to call the police. He would drop Jamie off at Joan's house to check inside again, then search all the woodland behind it. Patti had reminded him, too, of the trail that she and Joan used, that led from the old grey house, crossed the gravel pit land, and then came out by their own farm fence where the stream went under it. He would come home that way, searching as he came. They agreed it would be best for Mom to stay home, in case any one of them, or Joan, decided to telephone with news. She would phone Joan's house regularly during the afternoon.

After they had decided all that, it was Patti who suggested that none of them call out as they looked for Joan. After all, she wasn't *lost*, was she? In the bleak silence that had followed, they considered the difference between being lost—and running away.

Patti put Little Guy to a slow trot as they entered the woods. There was a network of old logging roads throughout this woodlot. Patti decided she would go over all of them quickly at first, scanning both sides carefully among the trees as she went. She was looking for any sign—a dropped piece of clothing, a pack showing a corner from behind a tree. Anything.

Where would *I* go, if I wanted to run away, Patti wondered. That's the question Mom had asked. Supposing I had some blankets, and cooking stuff, and some food? I *did* want to run away this morning, she interrupted her thoughts to remind herself. In a way, but just for a little while, not for keeps. And not long enough to worry Mom and Dad the way they were worried now. Maybe … maybe Joan would think about *them* soon, too.

Now she had come to the fence that crossed this road—time to turn back and cut across to the next logging road. No sign yet. Was she looking carefully enough? What if she found no sign at all? What if …

New thoughts were beginning to bother Patti, as she and Little Guy ambled deep into the woods again. Joan had no tent. What if it rained? What if it got cold in the night? And surely a loaf of bread and a few eggs couldn't last long. Lunch, probably. Supper, maybe. What then? And wouldn't she be lonely? Scared? Imagine having no family anymore. Imagine feeling unwelcome in the only family that was left to you!

Patti slipped out of the saddle and dropped the reins, knowing that Little Guy would stand if she told him to. She sat on a big rock and looked at her horse. Usually she told him all her problems and plans—but somehow, today, she just felt too bad to talk about it. He was quiet, though, and watched her as if he understood. It made her eyes blur with tears.

All around them, scattered among the big trees, were the pole-sized trees that Maynard had felled during the winter for the fencing Dad wanted done this summer. She and Little Guy would help him pull the logs out on to the road like they had done last summer. Soon, probably …

Oh, how she wished that she could think about ordinary, everyday things like that again!

But … but that was a kind of running away, too, wasn't it? How much running could a person do? Surely you had to just get on with a problem *some* time!

Yes. Patti wiped the tears from her face with the back of her hand and slipped off the rock. They had better hurry. It was mid-afternoon already, and it would get dark here in the woods much sooner than anywhere else.

Enough Space

"Just for a few minutes," Patti explained to Little Guy. This time she tied his reins around the trunk of a maple sapling and gave him a pat on the neck.

She had just had an idea: a camp. If Joan did indeed have the plan that Mom had suggested, well, a camp would need water, wouldn't it? Way back at the corner of this woodlot, where the fence divided their farm from three of their neighbours' farms, a good-sized stream ran through their property a short distance. It was close to the place where Jamie had been caught on some barbed wire a couple of years ago—the time that Patti had run for help. She would never forget that particular path! But it was blocked everywhere with snags and windfalls, so

Little Guy was safer here on the road while she worked her way through it.

"So, it *is* you!"

Patti jumped and whirled around to see a tall, thin, dark-haired figure peering at her through some especially tangled undergrowth. She let out a deep breath, and stood, speechless, while her heart pounded. Joan looked tired—her face was drawn and there were deep shadows under her eyes. But, what was this? There was a shine in those eyes that Patti hadn't seen in a long time.

"I hoped it would be you," Joan said, as she picked her way carefully through a mass of bush.

"I don't know why." Patti had found her voice, but her eyes were filling with tears again. "*I* was the one who said all those mean things."

"They weren't exactly *mean*," observed Joan in a very matter-of-fact tone, stepping free of clinging brush at last. "You only said what you really thought. And it just told me in a different way something I was already thinking."

"Like what?" asked Patti.

"Like, I don't belong in an ordinary family ..."

"Oh, that's not true!" cried Patti in dismay. "My family really likes you!"

"I know. I don't mean *that*." Joan had picked up a stick and was breaking off the small branches along its length as she thought about what to say.

"What I mean is ... you see, I've looked after myself

ever since I was little. What I'm used to is looking after the others. I … I don't think I *like* being looked after. Even by your folks. They're so nice … but … look, I know I make things harder for them. And you. Every day, I know it. I'm sorry. I tried … but I just can't be comfortable at your place."

Patti looked at Joan, helplessly, trying to think of the right thing to say that would fix this confusing situation— the kind of thing that Mom would say if she were here.

But the strange thing was, Joan didn't look the least bit confused. Or sad. She looked like someone whose mind was made up. "I'm going to make myself a cabin," she said, tossing the stripped stick into the bushes. "A *real* cabin this time. And I'm going to live here in the woods. Like a pioneer."

"But … what about food? What about … you don't have the right stuff to make a cabin, do you?"

"Well, not a *fancy* cabin," Joan admitted, reluctantly. "A stick cabin. I've already started it. I'll need some plastic, though, for when it rains. Want to see it? C'mon!"

Joan led Patti through the woods, along the almost invisible path that Patti had intended to follow. And there, near the stream, exactly where Patti had planned to look anyway, was the pile of Joan's belongings that she had been searching for.

"Did you hear me coming?" Patti asked.

"A mile away," Joan said with a toss of her head and a

sly grin. "I heard Little Guy mostly, so I thought it would be you. This is a good place, isn't it? I can hear someone coming and disappear into the woods long before anyone gets to the campsite." She laughed. "I'd better be careful not to make that path any better, eh?"

Patti nodded. But she was troubled. Everything had changed so quickly, her head was spinning. It was good to see Joan back to herself again, but ...

"If you heard me, why did you come to find me?" she asked.

"Because I need your help," said Joan. "Will you get stuff for me and help me build? It'll be fun!"

"But what about Mom and Dad? They're *so* worried right now! And they're going to phone Aunt Kate and the police if you don't turn up before dark!"

Joan was quiet. Some of the light seemed to have gone from her eyes. She shoved her hands into the pockets of her old jeans and sat down on a log.

"I don't want to worry them," she said at last. "I don't want to be any more trouble to them than I've been already." She looked up at Patti, thinking. "That's the biggest reason I need your help, I guess. So you can tell them I'm okay and not to worry. But ... if you tell them where I am, won't they *make* me go back? Can't you just tell them you *know* where I am? That I'm okay?"

Patti was remembering her parents' anxious faces— the way they had looked a short while ago, as everyone grabbed a peanut butter sandwich and headed out to search. What should she do? She absolutely had to put their minds at rest. Right away. Yet here was Joan, with a new hope and an exciting new project. Patti had seriously failed Joan once—would she have to do it again?

"I think …" she said, finally, "I can't promise, but I *think* Mom and Dad would let you camp in the woods, as long as they know you're safe."

"Really?"

"Well, they'll probably insist on a tent, and a tarp, and food, and all that sort of stuff. Mom will probably bring down a few three-course meals!" Patti laughed.

"No!" Joan stood up, her hands on her hips. Her face looked like thunder. "Nobody but *you* can know where I am! *Nobody*!"

Patti looked at her for a long time.

"Okay," she said. "Nobody but me will know where you are."

"I'm sorry, Patti. That's just not possible." Mom looked relieved, but also very decided. She thumped her chopping board into the sink to emphasize her point.

"Oh, *please*," begged Patti. She was feeling desperate.

This discussion had gone round and round in circles for the past half an hour. A stew was bubbling on the stove, which meant that supper was soon, but Joan was needing her before dark with some food and the plastic tarp from their playhouse, which was way down in the other woods. She was running out of time.

"You have to understand, Patti," said Dad for the umpteenth time. "We're responsible for Joan. She's an unusually competent kid, but she's still only twelve years old. Aunt Kate trusts us to treat her as if she were one of our own kids. Do you think we'd let you or Jamie be out there all by yourself, who knows where? You have to see it from *our* point of view!"

"I *do*," wailed Patti. "That's the trouble! I see it from both sides!"

"Has she got any water for her camp? A stream or something?" interrupted Jamie, suddenly. He was sitting at the table with Dad, while Mom was tidying the counters after chopping the vegetables for supper.

Patti nodded, wearily. The question surprised her, but she was happy to have a change of subject. She had found all three of them back at the house, worried and discouraged, when she and Little Guy came trotting up the driveway. At first, it was wonderful to be able to tell them the good news. To sit at the table with cookies and milk and listen to everyone's afternoon adventures, especially since it had all ended happily. But when she began to tell them about Joan's plans, well, that was the end of feeling good. With an absolute "no" on Joan's side and another "no" from Mom and Dad, there didn't seem to be anywhere to go from here. They were stuck. Would Joan run away again if Patti told her parents where she was? Somewhere this time, maybe, where she *couldn't* be found? How could she get Mom and Dad to see the danger?

"Tell her she should always boil the water," Jamie was saying in his bossiest, big brother voice. "Does she have matches?"

Patti looked at him in amazement. Why was he sounding so hopeful? Didn't he realize …?

"I … I guess so," she said, bewildered. "Maybe I should take her some more."

"At Scout camp we *always* boil the water," insisted Jamie, as if she had argued against his point. "Tell her it doesn't matter how clean it looks—it probably came through someone's pasture land far away. Cows and pigs and chickens and …"

"Okay, *okay*, Jamie," interrupted Dad suddenly. "We get your point."

"Do you *really*?" asked Jamie, giving his father a meaningful look.

What on earth? Patti looked from Dad to Jamie and back to Dad just in time to see him nod and give his son a little smile.

"What …" protested Patti, but Jamie interrupted her

again.

"Did you say you have to go back down tonight?" he continued, bossy again. "Before dark?"

Patti nodded, wide-eyed.

"Well then, we'd better figure out how you'll carry all the stuff she needs. And by the way, you'd better take my tent and forget your old piece of plastic. It'll do till she gets her shelter built—its old but the tarp is new. It'll keep out the rain. It'll take a while to build this stick cabin you're talking about."

"Thanks," Patti said, still puzzled. And then she said, "Hey, what …?"

Again Jamie interrupted impatiently. "How *will* you carry the stuff?"

"I … I thought, if Mom and Dad agreed … I thought I would harness Little Guy to the wagon. But …" She was so very tired and confused. So completely out of ideas.

"Perhaps …" Mom said gently, coming around to put her hands on Patti's shoulders. "Maybe you could take your sleeping bag and stay the night with her. I'd feel better if I knew she had some company tonight."

"Good idea," said Dad.

"But …" Patti looked from Mom to Dad, amazed. What had she missed? "I thought you said 'no'. I thought …"

"I guess we just changed our minds," said Dad. "People do that sometimes, you know." There was a sparkle in his eyes. "You're in a difficult situation, Patti, we can see that. And so is Joan. And so are we. The time has come for a compromise."

Mom sat down at the table and nodded. "We understand that Joan needs some space, honey," she said. "We just need to know that she's safe."

Jamie was looking very pleased with himself across the table. Patti stared at him for a moment. But Dad was talking to her again. "Suppose you offer Joan a deal tonight. You tell her that she can keep her camp a secret— but only for a few days. Maybe a week. We'll tell Aunt Kate when she phones tonight that you two are off camping and that Joan sends her love. But we can't go longer than that without telling her *exactly* what's going on. Your job is to help Joan to change *her* mind in that time—to think about compromise. Agreed?"

"Agreed," said Patti with a sigh. This wouldn't be easy. But it was sure a lot better than it had been just a few minutes ago!

Dad pushed his chair back. He came around the table and pulled Patti up to give her a very big hug. "Now," he said, "let's all of us help to get your things together, and some hot stew, and send you off camping!"

"What's *that* noise, then?" asked Patti.

"Dunno," answered Joan. "Another kind of owl maybe?"

"I'd better bring down a bird book," said Patti, rolling over in her sleeping bag so she could see the coals of the campfire glowing in the dark. Beyond the occasional crackle of the dying fire, she could hear the stream murmuring its way between rocks and steep banks.

"You'd better wait till we get the little cabin built," said Joan. "There's not much room in the tent to keep things dry."

That's true, thought Patti. Her pack and her clothes at the foot of her bed didn't even leave much space for feet.

They were both very tired, but much too excited to sleep just yet. By the time Patti and Little Guy had brought the wagon to the other end of the trail, and Patti had whistled for Joan to come and help, it was already dusk deep in the woods. They had constructed a corral of rope right there, and given the little horse half of the hay and water from the wagon.

"You'll be all right, won't you?" she had asked him. Rubbing his head against her stomach, he had given her a look that reminded her that Little Guy liked to do different and exciting things sometimes too.

"He'll be able to hear us talking," Joan had pointed out. "The woods are so quiet—it's surprising how far sounds carry."

The hardest part had been dragging the tent and tarp along what Joan called her "not-quite-path". They kept getting stopped by rocks and trees. Then, although it was well past suppertime and the girls were starving, they decided to make the most of what little light was left to choose a spot for the tent and get it up. Then they anchored the tarp securely over it.

"Rain can come up pretty fast in the night," Jamie had warned. "It's important to keep your bedding dry."

That's Jamie, lecturing again, Patti thought as she remembered. It was amazing how much of that she had patiently accepted from Jamie as he helped her pack and stow the camping gear in the wagon, then painstakingly wedge the pot of hot stew Mom had sent for their supper so that it couldn't possibly spill. She couldn't imagine *how* he had managed to get their parents to change their minds about keeping Joan's camping place a secret. All she knew was that he was a darn good person to have on your side when you needed someone!

"I'll have to get up in good time tomorrow," she said to Joan, sleepily. "I brought Little Guy's brush and stuff so I can groom him and feed him before we head for home."

There was no answer. Was Joan upset that she had to

leave so soon? "I simply can't be late at the stables," Patti explained. "But I'll come back down here as soon as I get back."

Still no answer. Patti raised her head to listen. There was only the gentle in and out of Joan's breathing.

It's a funny thing, she thought suddenly as she wriggled back down into her sleeping bag; only yesterday, her bedroom at home hadn't been big enough to hold Joan, herself, and all their things. Yet here they were tonight, together in one little tent—and it didn't seem too small in the least! They were friends again, and that's what made the difference.

Thunderstorm

It was hot and muggy. Towering black clouds loomed in the sky behind Patti as she pedalled furiously toward home. Where had this storm come from? It had been sunny and pleasant all morning at the stables, but now it would be nip and tuck to get home before the skies opened. It wasn't the thought of getting wet that bothered her, though. It was worry about Little Guy. He didn't mind rain, but he hated and feared thunder and lightning—and that's exactly what Patti suspected was on the way in those black clouds.

She got off her bike to walk up the final part of the steep hill on the outskirts of town, looking anxiously over her shoulder as she went. Oops, there it was, a great, jagged fork of light snaking down toward the trees in the far distance. A crack of thunder. A rumble.

Mom and Dad were at work. Would Jamie and Maynard think of Little Guy? Probably not—not if they had been caught by surprise, as she had. They were fencing today, down at the bottom field. Hang on, Little Guy, she muttered as she got back on her bike and whizzed along the flat as fast as she could go. A gust of wind caught at her back and pushed her on her way. Hang on, Little Guy, I'm coming!

And what about Joan, down in the woods? She'd forgotten all about her! She didn't know how Joan felt about thunder and lightning, but she would probably be rushing around right now, trying to get camping gear under cover before the rain hit. Too bad the girls had been side tracked from making the little stick cabin that Joan had planned, by the urgent need to get the rest of the camp in good order in time for parent inspection. Mom and Dad were getting very impatient about seeing the campsite; Patti had been promising it would be "soon" all week, and here it was, Friday already. It was almost a week since Joan had run away!

"How am I going to explain to Aunt Kate why Joan won't leave her camp in the woods long enough to talk to her?" Mom had complained last night when Patti came home from eating supper at the camp. "She's starting to wonder already, I can tell. I don't like not being completely truthful about this, Patti. The time has come for us to see the camp. Joan simply *has* to agree."

Joan did agree—in principle. "I guess I understand how your folks feel," she had admitted last night. "I'd probably feel the same. Maybe … what about the weekend? Sunday? Just so there's enough time to get this campsite so fantastic they'll let me stay!"

Looking around, at the tent, the plastic tarp shelter, the fireplace with its bench logs, Patti really hadn't understood what Joan was worrying about. Everything was tidy, in its place. Every day, when Patti had finished her work and lessons at the stable, and her farm chores at home, she had harnessed Little Guy to the wagon and loaded it up with all the things on the latest list. First there would be the things that Joan had asked for—like food, a hammer and nails, a shovel for the latrine—and then a longer list of all the things, like the cooler and more food, that Mom had just thought of.

Every day, as they ambled down the roadway toward the camp, Patti would wonder what Joan had cooked over the fire for their supper. Since that first night, Patti hadn't stayed overnight at the camp because she had to be up so early in the morning. But they always had the evenings together. And each day Patti was amazed at the changes Joan had made: a stick table, tied carefully together with the twine Patti had scrounged; a tripod for the fireplace, so Joan could tie Jamie's camping pot by its handle and hang it over the fire, instead of balancing it on some rocks; a stick cage for holding Mom's cooler in the stream bed, so the current wouldn't float it away. What new thing today, she always wondered. Joan's camp was fun.

There was such a change in Joan herself these days. Every evening she seemed more enthusiastic about the latest project, more eager to discuss the next one with Patti. What a pity it would be if things had to change when they were going so well. Mom and Dad were right, of course. Oh, I just hope this "inspection" goes well, Patti thought as she pedalled wildly around a bend and spotted their mailbox at the end of their long driveway.

A drop of rain coincided with another crack of thunder. The storm was getting close! Here I come, Little Guy! Stay dry, Joan!

Whoosh! It was like a bucket of water emptied on her head. The first big downpour. It soaked Patti before she could manoeuver her bicycle between the big barn doors. She ran through to the back door of the barn. And there was Little Guy, head down and sadly bedraggled, waiting for her beside the paddock gate. "You knew I was coming, didn't you?" she cried.

She led him into the barn and into his stall. He jerked his head with the next crash of thunder, his eyes showing white. Quickly, she reached to pull out the prop that held the stall's window shutter open, and fastened it down.

"It'll be dark for you," she explained to him, "but it'll

be a lot cozier. And you won't see that horrible lightning."

Then she gave him a rubdown with the old towel she kept in his stall, talking to him all the time. As he listened he began to calm down, and soon he was inching away from Patti toward the fresh hay in his feeding rack. Patti laughed, and gave his head a hug. "I'm going to leave you here for now," she told him. "I have to get myself dry too, and change, and find my rain cape, so I can go down to the camp and help Joan. I'll take my bike today, and take just what will fit in my basket. I think it's just bread and milk and eggs anyway. Oh yes, and the bag of apples I brought up from the cellar last night."

She knew Little Guy was still listening, though what he could hear over his munching and crunching she couldn't imagine!

The campsite was wet and empty. The rain rattled noisily above Patti on the tree canopy, but only a scattered pattering made it through to the soaked ground. Her shoes squelched as she walked. The thunder and lightning was moving away already, a steady rumble in the distance. Patti went to stand by the spitting fire; here and there among the burnt ends of wood, little curls of acrid smoke escaped. Gone was the welcoming, homey feeling she had come to expect in the camp. It was chilly and dreary. Patti shivered. She couldn't help remembering the warm, empty house she had left just a little while ago—the light on in the kitchen where she had left a note for Jamie, telling him where she was going.

"Joan!" she called.

"Here," said a muffled voice. The tent flap opened. "I should have put a shelter over the fire too," commented Joan, looking out, chin on her hands. "I never thought of it. Next project!" She looked warm and dry and cheerful under her blankets. "At least I managed to get all the firewood we collected under the plastic."

Patti looked around again at the wet and battered camp. Then she looked down at herself. In spite of her rain cape, her jeans were sticking wetly to her knees. Drops of water fell from her bangs and her nose. It had been a soggy business, pushing her way through the bushes from the logging road where she had left her bike.

"I hope we can make a proper trail soon," she said, "when your campsite isn't a secret anymore."

"Why don't you put the bag under the plastic shelter," suggested Joan. "C'mon into the tent. It's okay in here."

"I can't," exclaimed Patti. "I'll soak the blankets and my sleeping bag. I'm all wet!"

"Well …" said Joan, considering. "Take your cape off and drape it over the wood under the plastic. And your jeans too."

"It's still *raining*!" protested Patti, palms out to catch the drops. "How do I get from the shelter to the tent?"

"Run," said Joan, practically. "I'll hold the flap open when you're ready. Just dive in. But leave your feet outside till you take off your socks and shoes."

Things *did* look a lot better from inside the tent, Patti decided, pushing her feet deep into her sleeping bag and wriggling them to get them warm. With luck, the rain would soon stop completely and then they could make a big, hot fire. "Were you afraid of the thunder and lightning?" she asked, as a fresh wind shook a loud pattering of drops onto the tarp over their heads.

"Not inside here," Joan answered. "Not with the flap closed. But I *am* hungry."

"Uh oh," Patti remembered. "I left a whole bag of apples in the pack outside."

"I'll get them," Joan offered. She sat up to slip on her shoes. "One, two, three ..." The girls laughed as Joan landed with a thump against the woodpile, and then again as she charged head first back into the tent, her arms full of apples. This is like it used to be, thought Patti as she munched contentedly. The rain eased up for a few minutes, then came pouring down again with renewed strength. She remembered the games they used to play, whenever Joan could get away from her responsibilities at home. When it came to pretending, Joan was more fun than anyone she knew.

And then she suddenly had a surprising thought: I can only *think* about how it used to be—I can't *say* it to Joan. Not yet, anyway. This feels like one of our games, but it *isn't*. For one thing, Joan isn't the same. Me either.

And everything depends on Mom and Dad right now. Everything.

"Why are you so quiet?" asked Joan.

"Just thinking," said Patti.

"So … do you *think* your Mom and Dad will let me stay here in camp? Especially now that it's rained?" Joan's voice was quiet, troubled.

Patti paused before she answered. This was important. "Yes, I think so," she said finally. "Or … well, they'll think of something, even if it isn't *exactly* that."

She looked quickly over at Joan, who didn't look very reassured. "They *want* it to work, Joan," she explained. "The same way they want things to work out for Jamie and me. You're one of the family now."

Joan was staring out through the bottom of the flap. She didn't say anything for a long time. Finally she sighed. "I don't *have* a family anymore," she said.

There were no more words that were any use at all. How could Patti contradict something Joan believed so deeply? If only Mom and Dad could accept a secret campsite for a bit longer—just a bit more time might make all the difference. But how could she possibly persuade them?

As if to answer her mixed-up thoughts, a great wind suddenly swirled through the camp, battering at the trees, flapping the plastic shelter, caving in one side of the tent and billowing the other. The rain thundered down above them. Patti wriggled her toes, as she listened to the commotion outside. It seemed to be taking a long time to get her feet warm today. In fact … she pushed them right to the bottom of the sleeping bag experimentally. Hey! They were even wetter than before!

It took another moment for the whole truth to sink in. With a gasp, Patti lifted the tent flap and stuck her head out to check her suspicion. "Joan," she said in a choked voice, "you know that nice, sheltered little hollow we pitched the tent in …"

Horrified, Joan suddenly understood. "Oh no," she groaned. "Stupid me!"

Sure enough, as they lifted their bedding to check, they could actually see the water seeping through the seams of the tent floor. It wasn't just wet, there was a large puddle, and it was growing by the second.

"It's like pitching our tent in a *lake*!" cried Patti.

Now what? A discouraged silence filled the tent, while the storm raged outside. It obviously wasn't going to stop any time soon.

Thump, thump. Patti opened the flap again to hear better. A tree knocked down in the wind? Something in the shelter falling over? Feet along the path?

Feet!

The certainty hit Patti and Joan at the same time. They both reached to unzip the flap to the top.

"Hurry!" yelled a yellow-coated figure as it burst through the final clump of bushes to the camp clearing.

Jamie!

"Maynard's got the pickup at the turnaround!" he shouted over the racket of the storm. "Leave the tent and stuff—we'll come back for it when this is over! Hurry!"

Patti and Joan looked at one another. Then Joan sat up and began to pull on her shoes. "You'll have to bring me my jeans," Patti told her.

The two girls shared Patti's cape as well as two people can who are scrambling single-file along a bushy, wet, overgrown path. And then, huddling in the back of a pickup truck, beneath a cold and merciless rain.

An hour later, Patti broached the difficult question. The three of them—Jamie, Patti, and Joan—were sitting in the kitchen drinking hot chocolate. Each of them had had a hot shower and changed into fresh clothes. Joan borrowed some of Mom's, because Patti's were too small. Joan had seemed as grateful as the others to be in the warm house, which muffled the sounds of the storm outside. She had chattered away excitedly as they took turns in the bathroom, sorted through clothes to find some that fit, and boiled the kettle. But for the past few minutes she had been very quiet. Patti eyed her anxiously, then turned to

Jamie. "How did you *know* where we were?"

Jamie looked from Patti to Joan, then back to Patti. "Hey," he said, in a protesting sort of voice, "it wasn't *my* idea to come and get you, you know. Dad phoned from work soon after Maynard and I made it back from the bottom field. Maynard was going home—we'd decided to call it quits for the day. But Dad said first we should go and pick you guys up—and don't take 'no' for an answer." Jamie turned to Joan with an awkward laugh. "But I didn't hear a single one of those 'no's!"

"Oh!" exclaimed Patti impatiently, "I mean how did you know *where* we were. We thought it was a secret!"

Jamie looked at them both again. "Well …" he began reluctantly. He counted off points on his fingers. "A secret camping place somewhere across the road. Near a stream. Close enough for Little Guy to pull supplies in the wagon. And then, a familiar bike leaning against a tree at the beginning of an overgrown sort of path … But not as overgrown as it used to be."

"Oh," said Patti. So that was it. No wonder Mom and Dad had agreed to let the campsite stay secret for so long—they actually *knew* where it was! Of course they would guess. *She* had, hadn't she?

Jamie looked sorry that she felt so bad. "Hey Pats," he said, "don't forget, I know that place pretty well from past experiences."

Patti and Joan were silent. What was there to say?

Jamie looked uncomfortable. He checked the bottom of his empty cup, then he cleared his throat, as if to say, "here goes", and put his hands out on the table. "Dad gave me another message," he said. "Basically, I'm supposed to 'spill the beans' this afternoon. No more secrets."

He paused for a moment, while the two girls looked puzzled.

"You see, Dad and Mom and I have been talking about this stick house you guys are planning to build, and … well, it seems a pity to put so much effort into something that would be so flimsy and wouldn't last long."

"At least it'll keep out the rain," said Joan, coldly.

"Yes, I know, but …" Jamie was trying to find the right words. "You see, last winter Maynard cut too many poles. We've already just about finished the fences that Dad wants fixed, and there are still lots of the poles lying around in the woods. And that made us start thinking about the model cabin you guys made for school. Heck, you've already built a log cabin!"

A log cabin? Two sets of wide eyes stared at him across the table.

"Well, the truth is, Dad and I are really keen on this. He says he and Grandad built a little one when he was a teenager, and I … I'd be a big help. I want to learn how. And Dad says he has lots of stuff around the farm for a little cabin—like plywood, some leftover tin roofing and stuff. And …"

Jamie ran out of words. He was looking anxiously at the two girls. He knew that look on Patti's face—any exciting new project produced that look! But Joan. *Her* face was expressionless.

"So …" she said, her voice still cold. "You and your Dad want to build me a little log house?"

"No!" exclaimed Jamie. "No, no, no! Dad has to work, and I'm off to Scout camp in a couple of weeks. No, Dad will help you with the plans and teach you what to do as you go along. And I want to learn too, and maybe help you whenever I can."

Joan looked over at Patti, and Patti looked at Joan. A *real* log cabin! Could they do it? The question flew silently between them and Joan's face caught the excited Patti look.

And Jamie heaved a great sigh of relief.

Then the important questions began. Where? What first? How big? Out came the writing pad and pencils as ideas came and went and some got written down. Outside the summer storm raged, but nobody noticed it anymore.

More Storms

"This is *good*!" exclaimed Patti, sitting on the "settee" log in front of the fire. A last shaft of sunlight filtered through the treetops, lighting up the tent on its new site on the slight rise opposite her.

She grinned up at Joan, who was standing at her stick table, cutting up the bannock bread she had just cooked over some glowing coals. Patti's piece was crusty and well browned on both sides, and it was slathered with Mom's homemade butter and strawberry jam. "Dessert before first course," she said, through a last mouthful. "This is *my* kind of dinner!"

"Ready for the next one?" asked Joan with a glint in her eyes. Patti knew that look. She struggled to her feet.

"No, Joan! No! Not with jam ..."

But it was too late. Patti was up in time to catch the bannock as if it were a softball. Both hands. Joan laughed with delight at Patti's sticky red and yellow fingers.

They were back in camp at last. It had taken nearly a week to get their tent and bedding dry—for a few days it all had to be strung up in the basement, until the weather remembered that this was supposed to be summer. Then there were two more days with it all blowing on the clothesline in the sun and wind.

It had been a good week, though. Not at all like the ones before Joan ran away. Patti licked her hands and watched her friend. She was using the wooden cutting board that Mom had found in the basement, where so many of the extra things from Gramma's big house had been stored. There was a good knife too, better than the one that came from Joan's house. And some cookie tins—Joan was busy putting some of the bannock into one of them. When you camp in the woods, the girls had learned, you had to remember about mice, squirrels, raccoons, and flies.

Under the table stood three big pots with lids, useful for holding washing water and for boiling the drinking water if it came from the stream. The bannock recipe was one of many that Mom had taught Joan. Every day after work, Mom still flipped through her recipe books to see what else she could find that would be easy to cook over a campfire. Which is why a fragrant spaghetti sauce was at that very moment bubbling in Gramma's heavy cauldron.

"You need at least one heavy pot," Mom had explained. "You can't control a campfire the way you can a stove."

At first Joan didn't want it because it was too heavy for her stick tripod. But Dad found three pieces of pipe in his shop, and the girls made a stronger tripod from that with wire, so now the cauldron spent almost all its time hanging there.

Patti reached over to give the sauce a stir with the wooden spoon.

"Pièce-en-pièce."

Patti looked up, surprised.

Joan was saying these words to herself as she worked. "Pièce-en-pièce." Suddenly she realized she was thinking out loud. She grinned at Patti, a lopsided, embarrassed sort of grin. "It means piece on top of piece. Log on top of log. Neat, eh?"

Patti knew she was echoing Dad. This was the way he had explained it to them just that afternoon: it was a different way of building their new cabin from the way they had built their model. It was the way of the French pioneers, which is why it had a French name. First, you erect a series of upright posts around the outside, on the base log; then, you slip short logs between them, into a slot on the sides of the uprights. This forms the walls.

It was a good method if your logs were small, like the ones Maynard had already cut. It was also the best way if a person had to build the cabin alone because he could manage each log by himself.

"Since you girls are going to be doing most of this by yourselves," Dad had pointed out, "it's definitely the way for you."

Patti had stolen a look at Joan when he said that. Would she be pleased that they could do it themselves? Or would she be annoyed that Dad had already made up his mind?

Joan frowned. "Too bad we chose the *wrong* way for the model, eh Patti?"

"Now we get to learn *two* ways of making a log cabin," Patti interjected into the silence that followed. But she knew then that trouble was brewing and that it had something to do with the cabin. Lately, Patti had been getting used to the ups and downs of this new Joan; the jokes and laughter were great—the way Joan used to be—but now they were often followed by storms. Patti watched Joan now and prepared herself for one of them.

"The problem is …" said Joan, squatting and propping herself up against the log bench opposite Patti, so she could take over the job of stirring the sauce. She paused for a moment, struggling for the right words. "The trouble is … will this cabin really be *mine*?"

"What do you mean?" asked Patti.

"It's not really the different way of building that bothers me," she explained. "Actually, I think that sounds great. I like learning the new stuff and it makes sense. But … but …"

At last she looked at Patti. "Well, it's your Dad and Jamie—they're so *enthusiastic*! So … *positive* about what we should do!"

Patti was still waiting.

"They've spent hours drawing the plans and talking about them," Joan continued. "Like, your Dad explaining how the long slits in the stand-up logs are cut. And then showing me how the ends are made on the filler logs so they'll slip down between the uprights. Mortise and tenon joints, right? But then … *then*, he goes out and helps me do practice ones in the barn. Even though he's already behind in his chores. It's … it's all so *much. Too* much!"

Patti waited some more.

"I just wonder," Joan said, "if, in the end, the cabin is really going to be *mine*."

It was true, Patti reflected. Dad and Jamie *were* enthusiastic. They loved an exciting project just as much as she and Joan did. "But it's mostly just talk with Dad," she pointed out. "He has to go to work every day except weekends. Jamie, too, for much of the time. Except for the couple of work-bees we've planned, they don't have time for anything *but* talk."

Joan was still troubled.

"You and I will be doing most of it," Patti assured her. "Everything we can do without help. But we have to learn first—and Dad can teach us."

There was a long silence as Joan stared into the fire.

"Which reminds me," said Patti briskly, "we'd better get started clearing the cabin spot tomorrow afternoon and on the weekend. Then we have to haul the first bunch of logs out of the bush so we can peel them."

Silence.

"Oh, I almost forgot," added Patti quickly, "we need some flat rocks to put under the base logs before we can do anything on the cabin. Hey! We've got a lot of things to do if we want to be ready for the work-bee a week from Saturday!"

That got Joan's attention. "I could get started on that tomorrow morning while you're at the stables," she said. "If you'll show me, right now, that pile of flat rocks you told me about, I could bring them in with the wheelbarrow."

They took the spaghetti sauce off the fire for the short while they would be away, then Patti followed Joan along the trail out to the wagon road. She watched the tall figure work her way skilfully between the bushes and snags—all focus and business now. Whew! Patti allowed herself a tentative sigh of relief. One more cloud blown away.

But not for long.

It was dusk in the deep woods when the girls finished

their supper and clean up. Time for Patti to collect Little Guy and head for home.

"Do you *have* to go?" said Joan abruptly.

"But tomorrow's Friday," Patti said, surprised. "I can stay tomorrow night, though." She raised her eyebrows in question.

"Oh, it's just …" Joan waved her hand dismissively. "It's nothing. It's just … sometimes, at night, it gets a bit spooky down here. I'm glad about the cabin—that'll be better."

Joan—afraid? This was something new. "I wonder … do you think Little Guy could stay with me at night?" she asked.

"But he can't even come through here to the camp until we clear that overgrown path," Patti pointed out. "And I'd have to come all the way down here every weekday morning. To feed him and groom him. I wouldn't have time, would I?"

"But what if I clear the path tomorrow, before I do the rocks?" said Joan. "We have to do it right away anyway, to make room for the wheelbarrow. And the logs. We could make him a little pen with rope around the trees, couldn't we? Like you did that first night we camped? Then I could take him up to the barn every morning, and feed and groom him *for* you. If you showed me how."

Patti thought about that. She nodded slowly as the idea took shape; maybe it would work. Little Guy was excellent company, and *he* certainly wouldn't mind. In fact, spending time with Little Guy might just be the best thing for Joan. It would be for *anybody*!

Just then she heard him whicker from his tether out on the wagon road. Time for his supper, he was saying. "Why don't you learn to ride him too," she suggested as they headed for the trail. "You used to say you wanted to."

Joan looked doubtful about that.

"Come on," Patti coaxed. "Ride him back to the barn right now, while I lead him. Then I'll show you how I feed him and all that stuff. First lesson. I'll walk you back down to camp later, with the barn flashlight."

"Okay," agreed Joan. "Wait a sec while I go back and get my flashlight too."

In no time at all, they were back to laughing again. "This—is—fun," giggled Joan, bouncing along on Little Guy's back as she started her first trot. Patti smiled as she jogged along beside them. She remembered the first time she trotted on a horse herself, only a year ago.

"Will you teach me how to drive the wagon too?" asked Joan, catching her breath as they slowed to a walk on the hill to the road. Her face shone with anticipation.

"Good idea," said Patti. "Then you won't have to wait for me to come back from the stables to get on with hauling logs and stuff. You and Little Guy can do some of it by yourselves."

Joan liked that idea. She slid out of the saddle and

walked beside Patti, and they crossed the road and head-ed up the long, dusky driveway in companionable silence.

Then along came trouble again.

"Your family has done so much for me," Joan observed with a sigh as they opened the gate to the barnyard. They could hear Dad and Jamie talking to the cows in the big barn. "*Too* much," she added ominously.

Up and down. Sometimes Patti just couldn't keep up with the change of moods!

"Well," said Patti, determined to end the evening on a cheerful note, "you've just offered to do my morning chores for me."

"I've been thinking …" Joan hesitated. "Do you sup-pose your Mom would let me do some of *her* chores in the morning too? When I come up to the house with Little Guy, I could maybe wash the dishes or do some vacuum-ing. What do you think?"

"Oh …" Patti was thinking fast. "It *would* give her more time in the garden, before she went to work, and she would love that. But …" Getting mixed in with Mom's chores in the morning, especially on work days? This was beginning to feel like tricky ground all of a sudden.

"I'll ask her tonight," said Patti, giving Joan her most confident smile. "But don't you mention it till I say. Okay?" That would give me time to try to persuade Mom, Patti told herself. She was the problem solver these days, and that seemed to be her most important job, as Joan's mood swung from cloud to sunshine and back again.

"Maybe you could be just a little less *definite* about the cabin plans? As if you hadn't already made up your mind?" she had suggested to Dad after their planning session this afternoon. And to Mom, who was making up a bannock mix, "If you showed Joan *how*, she could do that by herself." And to Jamie, several times, "I think it would work better if you waited till you were *asked* to help!"

I'm a trouble-shooter, that's what I am, she thought. And it's not an easy job.

"Just do Little Guy stuff tomorrow," she suggested to Joan now. "I'll let you know about Mom in a little while."

When the barn chores were done, Patti and Joan set off down the lane at a run, toward the darkening field. "Hey, you two, it's getting late!" called Dad, on his way to the house with his bucket of milk. "I'm just walking Joan down to the camp," Patti stopped to call back. "I'll be back right away!"

"Twenty minutes!" declared Dad.

"Besides," laughed Joan, between puffs, "you're actually *running* me down to the camp!"

"I'm *racing* you!" shouted Patti, darting on ahead. She knew her advantage wouldn't last, though—not against Joan's long legs.

"It's going to be fun, isn't it?" said Joan a few minutes later, when they had both recovered their breath and were nearing the woods. "All the stuff we have to do, I mean.

Peeling the logs—I liked it when your Dad was showing us how. The way the draw knife slips the bark off."

An "up" time!

"Dad figures it's a good time to peel right now," agreed Patti. "The logs are shrinking in the warmth of summer, and that loosens the bark. What I like is the way the spirit level works. Jamie showed me today. When we lay down the flat rocks, we have to remember to use the spirit level to be sure they're all level with each other, ready for the foundation logs. It'll take some fiddling, he says."

"Lucky I was the one to chop the wood for the stove at home," said Joan. "It's made me good with the axe. Your Dad thinks I won't have any trouble making the stick-out parts on the ends of the filler logs—making them so they'll fit into the slots."

"Imagine when the roof goes on!" exclaimed Patti, getting excited. "A *real* cabin! And maybe we'll even make *real* furniture! Just think—once we were excited about making furniture for just a model cabin!"

There was a long, awkward silence as both girls re-membered how much had happened since that time.

Patti switched on the big flashlight to enter the woods. It made a tunnel in the darkness. "I guess there's really an awful lot of work to do," she said finally, as they made their quiet way along the trail. "It won't always be fun."

But Joan had nothing to say till they were almost at the end of the trail. "I can go the rest of the way by myself," she said then, her voice muffled.

"Oh no!" said Patti. "I'll …"

"I've got my flashlight," interrupted Joan. Patti could tell she had been crying.

"Joan …" But Patti didn't know what to say. And she couldn't leave Joan while she was upset, could she?

"It's okay," Joan said with a wave of her hand. "It's just that I sometimes wonder what kind of person I am. With Mom gone, and the kids gone …" There was a strangled sob. "I wonder if I *should* be having so much fun."

Patti stood helplessly and watched Joan's flashlight disappear down the trail toward her camp. This was the big problem, after all, a cloud that hung over everything. But there was nothing that Patti could do to solve this one.

Foundations

It was Sunday, the day to meet Dad and plan the size and shape of the cabin. Patti was nervous as they banked down the fire and put away the food. Would Dad remember to be tactful? Joan had worked hard, and she seemed to be pleased with how things were going. But it was like walking a tightrope these days; it wouldn't take much for them all to fall off!

What a week it had been. The clearing of the spot for the cabin had been a fairly simple job and now it was almost done. They discovered soon after they started working that the slight, flat rise they had chosen had probably been cleared some time in the past, maybe even built up a bit with soil from somewhere else, Dad had said. Once

Maynard had finished cutting the few small trees, there were only a few saplings left to be chopped down and fallen branches to pick up and put in a pile for a winter bonfire.

"Do you suppose there was a cabin right here long ago, close to the stream?" Joan had asked. "A settler's, maybe, like our model cabin?" The thought seemed to please her.

Much harder was the clearing of a wide path the short distance from the campsite to the cabin spot, for Little Guy and his wagon. Once again, the saplings thrusting skyward alongside the path were small, but there were so many of them! Maybe this had been a logging road once? Everything had to be cut down flush with the ground so neither they nor Little Guy could twist a foot on the small stumps, and so that the logs he was dragging couldn't get snagged.

Patti made a face as she remembered her own efforts at chopping them down with an axe one evening last week, while Joan was fussing with supper over the fire.

"The stupid thing won't cut!" she had called, hot and frustrated after fifteen minutes of energetic hacking. "Your axe isn't sharp enough, Joan!"

How Joan had laughed when she came to look at the chewed-up wood near the base of Patti's sapling. "It isn't the *axe* that isn't sharp enough!" she declared, grabbing it impatiently from Patti's hand. With three swift strokes, she cut neatly through the green wood, level with the forest floor.

"How did you *do* that?" Patti had grumbled. "Practice," Joan had answered, waving her away airily. "You'd better haul the cut ones, Patti, and let me do the chopping."

Patti shook her head and grinned at the memory. Joan might be anxious right now, as they shouldered their packs for bringing stores back from the house, but there had been several times during the past week when she had been as know-it-all and irritating as ever she used to be. Thank goodness for that, thought Patti, following Joan along their path. And let's hope we can keep it that way!

"I only have three pieces of plywood left after the barn repairs," Dad announced in his usual decisive fashion when Joan and Patti met him in the barn. "So *that* will have to decide the size of the cabin."

Oh, oh. Bad start, thought Patti, wincing. Couldn't he have asked if that was okay—or *something*?

"So, Joan ..." he continued, with a quick look at Patti's expression, "measuring time for you. The plywood is your floor, and I've laid them out side by side. You need to know the combined length and width of the three sheets, so you know how to mark your base logs for cutting next Saturday. Of course, we'll do a final measuring when we put them together on site. Let's see how big your pace is."

What on earth?

Joan was puzzled, but she made a big step, then looked at Dad questioningly.

"Try several steps now," said Dad, "but keep them comfortable—the way you would walk."

Joan did as she was asked.

"Now," instructed Dad, "begin exactly at the corner of the plywood floor, and pace along the length side, keeping the paces the same size. Start with your heel at the beginning edge, and end with your toe at the top edge. Patti and I will count."

Carefully along one side went Joan. She stopped a short way before the end. There wasn't enough room for another whole pace. What now?

"Ah," said Dad, "now you'll have to use your feet to measure instead of your pace. Put your heel against your toe, and that's one foot. Almost there! Now your next heel against your toe …"

Joan was laughing by then, and teetering, hand waving to keep her balance.

"Right!" Dad shouted suddenly, like a sports announcer. "Ladies and gentlemen, she's there! What's her score, Patti?"

"Five Joan paces, and one and-a-half Joan feet," Patti

yelled back, and they all laughed noisily.

"Okay. Well done. Now the width side."

Joan began again, pacing confidently this time. "Four Joan paces," Patti announced.

"And there you have it!" Dad said with another laugh. "No measuring tape to try to remember—just be sure you have your feet with you!"

Whew, thought Patti. So far, so good.

Now Dad pulled out his notebook and drew a diagram on an empty page. "You'll eventually have to add the measurement of two log *widths* to the two long logs. The logs go on the outside of the plywood, and overlap at the width ends. You see?"

Yes, they could see. Dad's drawings were a big help.

"But that can wait till you've decided which log goes where at our work-bee next Saturday. With any luck, if we're careful, we won't have to cut the plywood at all. So the cabin will be as big as possible."

Joan nodded. Then she looked back at the plywood laid out on the floor, and her face clouded.

"What's wrong?" asked Patti.

Joan looked at Dad, then quickly away.

"Come on," Patti insisted. "Let's have it!"

"Well … it looks so *small*," Joan mumbled, so quietly that Patti could hardly hear.

But Dad had heard.

"Ah yes, *that*," he said. "It's funny—that always seems

to happen when you look down at a floor that doesn't have its walls yet. It suddenly seems too small. Tell you what: you and Patti go and decide where the window and door should be, and where you want your beds. Then lie down, and I'll draw the beds around you with my carpentry pencil. Tried and true method for making floor plans!"

And that's what they did, while Joan's face became all smiles and excitement again. First, the right place for the window, which would fit into one of the long sides. That window, Patti knew, was in the barn at this very moment, leaning up against a hay bale beside the door that Dad had already found. Both of them had lain in a pile of lumber in an abandoned chicken house for as long as she could remember. Their glass panes were long gone, their paint was peeling and they were a sad, dusty sight still. Patti knew that Dad had plans for their restoration: since things were going well, she had decided not to mention them to Joan just yet.

"Now," said Dad, as he finished sketching the bed outlines around them, "how about finding the right place and pretending you're sitting at the table?"

"Tea party!" Patti joked as they sat cross-legged on the floor while Dad drew their table and chairs around them. She was so happy to see Joan's answering grin, and to hear her say to Dad as they stood to inspect the results, "You're right, Mr. Blackburn. That's plenty big enough."

"How about calling me Bob," he answered gently, with

a twinkle in his eye. "No one but my bank manager calls me Mr. Blackburn, and that makes me nervous."

Patti caught his eye and smiled her thanks.

"Does it look all right?"

"Of course!" Patti glanced briefly at the freshly cooked bannock Joan had set on her table, then she turned back to tidying the tent.

"It isn't too *brown*?"

Patti stopped to look again, this time at Joan—she had never known her to be so fussy! But then, this was Saturday, the work-bee day, and Mom and Dad and Jamie were expected in about fifteen minutes to check out the camp, and start the work. Joan was treating it like some kind of military inspection.

"It'll make a perfect mid-morning snack," she assured her friend. "Lemonade too?"

Joan nodded anxiously. "It's in your Mom's big thermos already."

The campsite was immaculate. Joan had even raked the scuffed dirt patches around the dying fire. Little Guy had been groomed till he shone. He watched them now with ear-twitching interest from his small rope pen near the clearing for the new cabin. He liked being so close to the action, Patti decided—spending the nights and many of his days here with Joan suited him just fine.

Last evening they had brought his morning hay with them in the wagon, along with Dad's chainsaw and the other tools they would all need. It was still not quite eight o'clock on a sunny morning and Patti was happy with how things had worked out so far. She just wished that Joan would relax—Mom was bound to be pleased with what they had done.

Patti sat back on her sleeping bag and remembered their discussion last Sunday. She was glad she had talked to her parents earlier about Joan's worries that they were doing too much for her and that she wasn't being independent enough. They had taken those worries seriously, thank goodness, and that was one reason they had decided not to spend the whole day on the cabin work-bee—so that it wouldn't pile more obligation on Joan.

"Balance," Mom had said thoughtfully. "Let's focus on balance. Joan knows how precious a Saturday is to our farm, when we have to work in town all week. Let's just work at the cabin half-day—maybe till one o'clock? And the rest of the day you and Joan can help me weed and thin my carrots. That'll make her feel better."

Patti could hear the family, now, chattering as they came along the path. She scrambled out of the tent, tying back the flaps so everyone could see how tidy it was.

"Wow!" exclaimed Mom when they all finally burst into the campsite clearing. "Look at this! You girls have done a wonderful job!"

Everything had to be admired then: the fireplace, the stick furniture, the tent, and the neat stack of firewood. And next they moved on to inspect the cleared path to the cabin site, the peeled foundation logs and upright logs, and the flat rocks outlining the cabin-to-come.

"You've done such a lot in a short time," said Dad. "Let's see if *we* can do as well today." And with that, he swung his chainsaw off the wagon and set to work. First, he cut out a notch at both ends of each of the measured foundation logs so they would fit together. The saw roared and sputtered while the others watched, then they all worked together to haul each log over to its place. Then, after the side logs had been settled securely into the end logs, Jamie found the spirit level and checked them. Mom and the girls were his crew—they lifted the end of one log so he could shift a couple of the flat rocks just a little bit. "That's the only one not quite level. It probably settled during the week," he said generously.

Next, Mom, Joan, and Patti measured and marked the spot along the foundation logs where each upright log would fit—one on each corner, two along both the back and front sides of the cabin to frame the door and window. Eight logs in all. Then, with a hammer and chisel each, they settled down to chip away the wood to make a flat place for the end of each upright to sit. Dad had already made a series of downward cuts at every spot, so the work was easy and fun. The chips flew in the dappled sunshine.

Meanwhile, Dad finished cutting the uprights to their exact length, while Jamie dragged them, one at a time, over to the cabin site. There, Dad carefully cut a slit, three fingers wide, down the length of each upright, into which the ends of the filler logs would eventually fit. Once again the chainsaw roared and smoked, and long curls of pine littered the ground.

Jamie stood and watched in admiration as Dad finished the last log. "Just one try," he begged. "I know I can do it."

"Okay," said Dad, taking off his ear protectors to hand over, "just one try—on one of those waste pieces over there."

"What about the goggles too?" suggested Mom, standing up from her work to watch.

"Oh. Right." Dad slipped them over his head and gave them to Jamie. Then he propped one of the discarded log ends against another log and handed the chainsaw to Jamie.

"Are you going to *let* him use it?" complained Patti. "I thought you said we had to be sixteen to do that!"

Jamie made a face at her through the plastic goggles. "One try isn't *using* the chainsaw," he argued.

"Well," explained Dad, "I guess the main thing is being strong enough to hold it safely. Just be careful, Jamie." Mom and the girls crowded around to watch, while Dad talked Jamie through a straight cut, then a diagonal one, then a notch. Then Jamie tried a few on his own.

"Look, it's a face!" cried Mom suddenly, as the haze of blowing sawdust and smoke cleared for a moment.

"Yeah, I see it!" agreed Patti. "And that's got to be a hat on a head—sort of cone-shaped!"

Jamie had stopped cutting to see what all the excitement was about.

"And that's almost a beard, isn't it?" said Joan, joining in the game.

"I think it's a gnome trying to crawl out of that log," said Mom with a laugh. "Look—it's *got* to be a gnome. Hey … a *house* gnome!"

"What's that?" Patti looked at Mom in surprise.

Mom laughed an embarrassed sort of laugh. "Oh, it's just … just …"

She waved the question away as Jamie went back to cutting.

"Hey, Jamie," cried Patti, "don't ruin it—it's a gnome we've got there! Don't cut off its hat!"

"That's enough for today anyway," said Dad, moving in to reclaim his equipment.

"For *today*?" asked Jamie hopefully.

"Till you're *sixteen!*" said Dad.

"How about cutting the gnome off the log?" asked Patti. "So we can set him up somewhere and finish him later?"

"Do we get our bannock and lemonade any time soon?" asked Dad, after he had watched first Mom and then the two girls add a few careful cuts to the gnome with their chisels and hammers. It had the beginnings of two large eyes under bushy brows. It was magic, Patti thought, as she glimpsed the face beginning to emerge from the hacked piece of log. Dad had carried it to a stump near the campsite so its eyes were almost at a level with Patti's. She stared at it.

"I'll put the food out now then, okay Joan?" suggested Mom, handing over her tools to an eager Jamie. He had already spotted a possible ear, and Joan was preoccupied with that.

"No, no!" Joan cried, as he prepared to hit the chisel with the hammer. "Higher! A little higher!"

She's forgotten to worry about her food, thought Patti suddenly. She has completely forgotten all the things that were bothering her. And that was a kind of magic too.

Mom and Dad had settled down on one of the "settee" logs with a full plate and cups when Patti trotted down the path to join them, stopping to give Little Guy a rub as she went past. In a few minutes, Jamie and Joan trooped in too. They made a contented circle around the campfire ashes in the cool shade of the big maples, their mouths full of bannock and jam.

"Well, I suppose we'd better get back to cabin work," said Patti soon, a bit regretfully. "I guess a house's foundations need to come before a house gnome—whatever that is!"

The others murmured in agreement and started to get up. Except for Mom who had been gazing off into the woods, a preoccupied look on her face. She turned to look at Patti, surprised, thoughtful.

"Maybe …" she said, then stopped.

"Maybe what?" asked Patti.

Mom stood up too, and laughed. She waved the question away as if it were chainsaw smoke, and started collecting the plates. That's the second time she's done that today, mused Patti. What's going on with Mom?

"Come on, Mom, what *is* a house gnome?" she asked. "Tell us."

"It's a kind of spirit, I guess," Mom said, reluctantly, after thinking a moment. "A protective sort of creature. A *good* thing for any house to have, anyway." She laughed that embarrassed laugh again.

"Does a house *gnome* have a *name*?" asked Joan, her eyes alight with fun. Or was she helping Mom out of a tight spot?

"Ha!" shouted Jamie. "A gnome name!"

"Gnome sweet gnome!" joked Dad. "Get it? Home sweet home!"

"There's no place like gnome!" sputtered Joan, her tanned face flushed with giggles. They all laughed with her.

Through her own laughter, Patti was still wondering about Mom. There was something serious behind this. What could it be?

Gnome Sweet Gnome

"Okay, crew," announced Dad at last. "Enough comedy. Time to plan the next stage of work."

The late morning sun filtered down on the smouldering fire as they licked the jam off their fingers and clustered around him. It was beginning to get warm, even here, deep in the woods; Patti peeled off her sweatshirt. Then she turned her whole attention to Dad.

"What we need to do next," explained Dad, "is to drill a hole in the middle of each of those flat spots you girls have chiselled out on the base logs. The hole needs to be half the length of those short steel rods Maynard and I cut the other day. They're called "rebar". I wrapped them in a rag and put them on the wagon last night, beside the tools. I'll get you to bring them to us in a few minutes, Patti."

Dad leaned forward now, his hands busy demonstrating how they would use the rebar. "We'll push one down into each drilled hole. Then we'll drill a corresponding hole in the end of each upright log. Finally, we'll lift up the log and slip the hole in the log over the sticking up part of the rebar. That's to stop the uprights from ever shifting sideways under the pressure of the filler logs.

"Jamie, I'll give you the job of using the brace and bit to do the drilling, since you've used it before. And Patti, you'll be his assistant. You need to be careful with the measuring, okay? And you might need help when it's time to push the logs right down over the rebar." He turned to Joan. "Meanwhile, you and I will nail those two-by-six boards over there around the inside of the foundation logs to support the joists. They need to be absolutely level."

"Or else the floor will slant," said Joan, her eyes alight with interest. "But what are joists?"

"They're the next level—the boards that go across the width of the cabin to support the plywood."

"And they need to be level too!" said Joan.

"Right," said Dad with a smile. "Let's see: we already carried the three pieces of plywood over to the site, didn't we?" The two girls nodded. That had been one of their jobs yesterday.

"Then, Helen," he said, turning to Mom, "would you

bring the five joists from the wagon? You'll see them in a bundle next to the toolbox. They're the long ones, in the best shape. Can you manage that—maybe one at a time?"

Mom nodded. "I'll use the wheelbarrow," she said.

"After that, if everyone else is still busy, would you bring the other reject lumber over so we can use them as braces for the uprights? We need to have them absolutely solid so that Patti and Joan can peel the filler logs by themselves whenever they have time, and slip them down between the uprights."

Mom nodded again, absently. Then, he turned to Patti and Joan, and they nodded too, to show that they understood.

For the next hour or so, everyone was busy. Patti and Jamie concentrated on their project on the outside of the cabin frame: the hole in the base log had to be in the exact centre of each flattened spot, and so did the matching hole in the bottom of each upright log. Patti worked with the ruler and the carpenter pencil, while Jamie turned the brace and bit, keeping the hole as straight as he could. Meanwhile, they could hear Joan and Dad on the inside.

"How does that look on the spirit level?" Dad would call from one end of a board.

"A tiny bit lower," Joan would answer. "A bit more! There! That's it!"

Then there would be the sound of two hammers at once, the whole cabin frame vibrating under Patti's pencil and ruler.

"Okay—next one!" Dad would say the moment the hammers stopped.

Meanwhile, the pile of boards from the wagon slowly grew just beyond Patti's view—she could judge Mom's progress by the great clatter whenever she dumped each load. Now and then she wondered why it took Mom so long *between* loads. When she looked up once to see, a clump of trees blocked her view of the wagon and the campsite. Was she stopping to clean up something there? But … what was there *left* to clean? Patti shook her head and went back to her measuring. Mom and Joan were both fanatical about cleaning these days.

As soon as they had finished the rebar holes and the curlicues of wood had been brushed away, Dad asked Patti and Jamie for help bringing over the plywood. It was heavy; whenever Dad and Joan dropped their hold on it for a moment to climb into the cabin frame, Patti strained to hold up her end until Dad could reach over and take it from her. Three times they did this. And then they watched with excitement as Dad and Joan manoeuvered each piece into place.

When the last piece was close to fitting, Dad and Joan had to climb out of the cabin frame. Then they pulled the plywood the rest of the way and settled it into place. Dad walked around the outside, checking each side and end carefully. At last he turned to the three waiting youngsters, with both thumbs up.

"Perfect," he cried, "not a single cut needed!"

"Yay!" they all yelled. The floor was on!

Mom suddenly emerged from under the trees near the campsite. "What's happened?" she called.

"We've got the floor on," yelled Patti. "It's *beautiful*!"

"Now, Patti and Jamie," said Dad, sounding business-like, but looking just as excited as the others, "suppose you leave your job for now and we'll help you finish up when we've got this floor nailed down. There are at least two more hammers on the wagon." He turned around.

"Helen …" He looked over at Mom's pile of boards, then all around the cabin site. "Now, where on earth …"

"She's probably getting another load," suggested Jamie.

"Helen?" Dad called louder.

Once again, Mom appeared from under that clump of trees. She had a funny expression, Patti thought—like when she's trying to hide Christmas presents.

"Will you bring two more hammers with your next load?" he asked. Mom nodded, then vanished again.

The others just had time to climb up on to the plywood floor and begin to imagine what it was going to look like, when Mom reappeared on the path, carefully balancing some long boards on the wheelbarrow. She must have had it all loaded and ready to go.

"How are you managing with that job?" Dad asked

when she reached them. He sounded a little worried. "Do you need some help? Maybe Patti ..."

"Oh *no!*" exclaimed Mom quickly. "I've got a system going here ..." she nodded emphatically, "a very *good* system, if I say so myself. Just one more load, anyway, and it'll be finished."

"Are you *sure*?" Dad asked again, sounding puzzled this time.

"*Definitely* sure," answered Mom. "Now let's have a look at that wonderful floor."

For the next half hour, a deafening noise dominated the little clearing deep in the woodlot, as four hammers nailed the plywood firmly into place. Patti rocked back on her heels once to listen. She chuckled as she thought about the birds and little creatures hearing all this hullabaloo—this was more noise than the chainsaw. She noticed that Dad, Jamie, and Joan were all smiling too as they worked, each trying to out-bang the others.

And then it was quiet. Such a quiet! They all stood up to feel the solid floor beneath them.

"No wobbles," announced Joan.

They all nodded and grinned at one another.

"And now for the uprights," said Dad.

At that moment, Mom appeared on the path with her last load of lumber. I should have helped her after all, thought Patti—it has taken her so *long*.

Mom looked cheerful, though. Very pleased with

herself, in fact. "Would you look at that!" she exclaimed admiringly, after she had dumped her boards. "The floor! You can believe in a cabin, can't you, once you've got yourself a floor."

She stood and watched as the crew lifted the first upright, standing on the new floor. Carefully, they eased it over its rebar, Jamie guiding it at the bottom. Then it stood up all by itself, held by the rebar, though it leaned a bit and swayed when anyone touched it.

"We'll put them all up first," said Dad, "and then we'll do the bracing."

There were eight uprights, all exactly measured to the height of the walls. It was a strange sight: a floor, surrounded by all those leaning poles. As they stood back to admire it, Patti saw Dad look around in a furtive sort of way. And then she realized that Mom was missing again. She caught Dad's eye, questioning.

But he said to her quickly, "Just *one* more job to do today, Patti. First we'll nail two braces on each upright … then hammer the stakes firmly into the ground …" and he wandered off, still talking. He knows what Mom's up to, thought Patti. And he doesn't want me to ask about it.

In a moment the clearing was full of noise again. Joan sharpened the stakes that Dad had cut with her axe, and Dad chose the right places and banged them into the ground. Patti and Jamie carried the long boards from the pile and nailed one end into the upright logs, while Dad made sure the other end of each board reached a stake. Each upright needed two boards to brace it, and each extended away from the cabin so they wouldn't get in the way of Patti and Joan as they fitted the filler logs later.

"Now," said Dad, "do we have both spirit levels? Patti and Joan will use them—one to check that each log is absolutely vertical from side to side, and the other to check forward and back." Dad demonstrated with one of the spirit levels. "The bubble has to be exactly in the centre for both directions, before Jamie and I nail the braces into the stakes."

It took Patti and Joan a few minutes to get the hang of it, but then things went quickly. Soon they were all standing together once more, admiring the frame of Joan's cabin.

"A skeleton," declared Patti. "Just the bones, waiting for its skin."

"That's it, all right," said Dad, putting an arm over the shoulders of each girl. He grinned over at Jamie. "Well, son, time for us to bow out until we have the next work-bee. I guess that'll be when we put on the roof."

"Pity," said Jamie wistfully, as he looked at the cabin. "Just when we were on a roll." But he grinned good-humouredly back at Dad.

"Oh, well," said Dad, "we working men …"

"Wow!" It was Mom, appearing again beside them. "It's done!"

Joan heaved a great sigh of satisfaction. "I think I *do* really believe in the cabin now," she said. "And I can't wait to get on with the next part of it."

"Lunch first," said Mom. "Let's get all this stuff back to the wagon."

When they had loaded the wheelbarrow with tools, Jamie pushed it along the path toward the camp. Dad carried his chainsaw and fuel behind him, and then came Joan with her axe. Patti followed her with Dad's satchel of hammers and nails. She turned to see Mom, still standing and staring at the cabin. "Aren't you coming, Mom?" she called.

Mom waved. "I'll be right there!"

Patti ducked under some branches into the camp clearing, and saw a strange sight: Dad, Jamie, and Joan were standing, frozen, their mouths open. Patti looked where they were looking, and her mouth fell open too. There, sitting on one of the settee logs, surrounded by a drift of wood chips and shavings, was the gnome. Mom must have carried him there on the wheelbarrow. Only now, he was a *real* gnome, not just a possibility. He stared right back at them, a curious yet friendly look in his eye. Patti was sure she could see a twinkle there. His cheeks were round and jolly, his lips almost hidden in a luxurious moustache and beard. Folded together over a fat little tummy, his hands were strong and capable, each knuckle knobbly and distinct. He stood confidently, his sturdy legs slightly apart and the soles of his boots melding into the log he was standing on.

Mom did *this*? So, *this* was her secret! Patti saw a hammer and chisel almost buried in the curls of wood.

Dad turned as Mom came into the campsite. Patti saw with amazement that he looked almost ... were those tears in his eyes? "Well, Helen," he said, as he went to put his arms around her. "I guess this means it's time for us to dig those tools of yours out of the trunk, eh?"

Mom looked pleased. "Yes, I think so too. For one thing, the gnome needs some fine finishing. I've gone as far as I can go with the rough chisel."

"*What* tools?" demanded Jamie, looking from one to the other.

"Your Mom used to be a carver, before you guys were born. Remember? We've told you about that, I'm sure. Lots of times. Her tools are still packed away."

"But ... but you've never done anything that *we've* seen," protested Patti.

"No," agreed Mom, smiling. "I guess I gave all my pieces away. Then, after we moved to the farm, there never was a spare moment for carving, what with chores, and you kids, and the job at the bank. I got completely out of the habit of thinking about it. But when that gnome started to grow out of his log, he just couldn't be ignored! It was so much fun, I've decided from now on to make more time for such things—they're important too. When

I really thought about it, Patti, I couldn't agree with you that a cabin's foundations should come *before* its house gnome. Or that everyday work should *always* come before the fun things."

Dad gave her a hug, and she grinned up at him. Then she winked at Patti.

Turning to Joan, she said, "A house needs walls of course, but I think it needs a spirit just as much. It needs to be *alive* to be a real home. The gnome is yours, Joan, to give your cabin a spirit and a protector—so it can always be your special home when you need it."

Patti looked back at the gnome. How *alive* it looked! And because of him, something had changed with Mom today. Something important. And later on, when Mom had finished the gnome, Joan's cabin would always have company, a friend down here in the woods, even when nobody else was here.

Joan squatted down in front of the gnome to see him more closely. Then she nodded solemnly up at Mom. She understood too.

"And now," said Mom briskly, "how about lunch and that carrot patch!"

Rustlers

It was a hot day, near the end of July. About a week till haying, Patti guessed, as she walked along the wagon road between fields of waving grasses. She pulled her t-shirt out of her shorts and flapped it vigorously to dry the sweat where it had bunched around her waist.

On the slight rise in the bottom field, on the way to Joan's camp, she stopped in surprise. An electric fence had appeared since yesterday in the far corner of the hay field, making a small enclosure right up against the woodlot.

"Dad's cattle," she said out loud. She watched them grazing quietly on the ripe hay, one black and white, and the other a golden brown. They had been out of her sight, down near the woods on the other side of the road since early spring. She was surprised to see how fat and sleek they had grown.

Patti thought she knew why Dad had moved them; lately, several of his friends had had one or more of their cattle disappear in the night. The thieves had left no clues, except for the tire tracks of their truck, and they were very quiet as they went about their business. Like most small farmers, Dad needed these cattle that he could fatten— after he had butchered one in the fall and put it into the family freezer, he could trade the extra one for someone else's surplus grain or lumber. Best of all, if he could sell it, there would be extra cash to cover any problems during the winter.

This must be a safe place, hidden so well from the road, Patti guessed. If such a thing existed as a safe place from those cattle thieves. Rustlers, Dad called them. Most of the stolen cattle had been taken from fields in sight of the road and the farmhouses, but some had disappeared from quite sheltered places too. Fences had been found clipped with wire cutters, or pushed down, and the cattle had been driven out to a truck on a side road. It made her angry to think anyone would do such a thing; farmers worked hard to keep up their fences and raise healthy animals. But what could they do about it?

Patti sighed as she turned to follow the road into the woods. Oh well, there was the cabin to think about, and

they *could* do something about that! It was Friday afternoon, which meant that she and Joan had two whole days
ahead of them to work on it together—maybe they could
get at least two more rounds of logs slipped into place this
weekend. Lately they had become very efficient at peeling
the logs that Little Guy and Joan had dragged to the cabin
from among the trees. Especially after Maynard had come
down to check on their progress. He offered to cut all the
logs to the right length with the chainsaw before they had
even peeled them. "No point in peelin' what you don't
need," he had pointed out. "Waste of time!"

He had stood for a few minutes, scratching the top of
his head and admiring the cabin so far. It looked wonderful, with four rounds of filler logs already dropped
between the uprights. The peeled wood glowed in the
sunlight. You could see how beautiful it was going to be.

"Doggone!" Maynard had exclaimed. "*Doggone!*"

Patti smiled as she remembered. She knew that was
his highest possible praise.

She started to jog eagerly now, along the cleared roadway to the camp. She had just figured out that when they
had six rounds of logs finished, they would be nearly a
third of the way up the walls. Let's see now—if it took two
weeks to get that far, then …

"Stick 'em up!"

Patti swivelled, mouth open, heart pounding.

"That's not *funny*," she exploded, as Joan appeared,

laughing, out of the shadows.

"Oh, yes it is," chortled Joan. "You didn't get to see your face!"

Patti groaned, then allowed a grudging smile. How many times had Joan done that to her? Today her friend's face was flushed, brimming with excitement.

"Did you get lots of logs ready today, then?" Patti asked, as they continued along the path. It was cooler here under the trees. "Nope," answered Joan. "Little Guy and I pulled a few to the cabin, but I spent most of the morning helping Maynard and Jamie put up that fence for the cattle. Good place for them, eh?"

"I couldn't see them at all from the road," Patti agreed.

"That's not the only reason, though." Joan looked very pleased with herself. "Maynard says that your dad chose it because you and I go up and down those big fields often enough every day—Little Guy and the wagon too—that it should put off anyone sneaking down here to find them. He says it's a lucky thing I'm camping down here this summer."

No wonder Joan was looking so happy, Patti thought. She nudged her as they came into the campsite clearing. "Do you reckon you could get your mind off those exciting rustlers long enough to do a blitz on a few logs?"

She checked her watch. "Two o'clock. We could work like crazy till suppertime—maybe get a head start on the weekend?"

"Just the same …" Joan interrupted herself to start using the swede saw, making the first short cut on one end of a log—her first step in making the tongue that would allow it to slip down between the uprights. "Just the same," she continued over the rasp of the saw, "I can't help hoping we might get *some* action from those rustlers."

She rolled the log over on the sawhorses so she could make the second cut.

"Rustlers!" she muttered to herself again. Patti could tell she liked the sound of the word.

"Don't get your hopes up." Patti was sitting astride a log propped up on two other logs. She pulled her drawknife toward herself, peeling the bark off in long, satisfying strips. "Exciting stuff like that never happens to us," she said, head to one side as she admired the sheen on the freshly peeled wood.

Patti was the first to wake up that night.

"That was Little Guy!" she whispered into the dark tent. "Did you hear him?"

"Wha'?" mumbled Joan.

The girls, tired out after working on the logs till dusk,

had gone to bed early, and they were sound asleep while it was still light outside.

"It's Little Guy," repeated Patti. "There's something wrong!"

Both of them heard it the next time—a low, muttered whinny.

"He never does that," exclaimed Patti, wriggling out of her sleeping bag. "There *must* be something wrong!"

When Patti crawled out of the tent, she could just see her horse, a dark shape against the starry sky. He twitched his ears and tossed his head as she stumbled toward him through the deep shadows of the moonless night. He was glad to see her.

"What is it, old fella?" she soothed quietly, rubbing his nose. "Have you got a stomach ache or something?"

Little Guy pulled his head away from Patti, alert, eyes white in the darkness, ears turned toward the farm. He whickered.

But Patti had heard it too.

"It's a car motor! Close!" exclaimed Joan, right behind Patti. Her blue pyjamas glowed a little in the starlight.

"Sh-h-h-h!" whispered Patti. She reached to grab her horse's halter. "We have to keep him quiet," she said urgently. "If it's those rustlers, and they're in the field next to the woods, they might hear him!"

"The cattle!" Joan whispered too this time. "I forgot about them!"

They listened again, intently. There it was again—the hum of a motor nearby, much closer than the main road.

"I'm sure it's there in the field," said Joan.

"I need to tell Dad." Patti put her face up to Joan's ear. "Right away. D'you think you could talk to Little Guy and keep him quiet, if I run up to the farm?"

"But … but …" Joan shook her head. "Your folks have gone to the dance, remember?" Oh, yes. The community dance. Mom and Dad didn't go often, but that's where they probably were right now.

"What time is it?" Patti asked.

Joan stumbled back to the tent, switched on her flashlight for a moment. "Eleven-thirty," she whispered, when she made it back to Patti.

"Is that all?" Patti was silent for a moment—Mom and Dad would still be at the dance. "But Jamie's at the house," she remembered, "and his friend Pete. We can call the police."

"It's so dark—you'll have to use your flashlight." Joan was troubled. "Won't the rustlers see you?"

Patti thought about that. "It'll be worst in the woods," she reasoned. "I can shield the flashlight—be sure I don't flash it around. When I get to the open field, I can wait till my eyes get used to the dark. I think I can see better already," she said, looking around and up at the sky which she could glimpse through the leaves. "But what if the truck comes up behind me when I'm still in the field?" A frightening thought.

"You could lie down in the tall hay beside the fence and just wait for them to go," suggested Joan. "You know, if you put on your jeans and the dark sweatshirt, they won't be able to see you."

Patti nodded. Quickly she disappeared in the direction of the tent, while Joan kept whispering nonsense into Little Guy's ears.

"Hey, Patti!" she whispered loudly when she saw a dark form heading toward the path. "I've got to hurry," protested Patti when she came back to Joan.

"Watch for someone on the lookout—maybe up by the main road," Joan warned. "You might not be the only one not using a flashlight."

Patti hadn't thought of that. She wondered: was this really the right thing to do?

"Dad always tells us to stay well away from anyone trying to steal something," she said. "He says that's the most dangerous situation to be in. It's better to just let them get away with the stuff."

She hesitated, uncertain. "I'll be careful," she promised. "I'll make sure they don't see me. But you be careful too—they mustn't hear you either, okay?"

"Who is it?" Jamie's voice was loud in the main kitchen, as Patti eased shut the screen door of the summer kitchen.

Suddenly the light switched on over her head.

"Turn it off!" exclaimed Patti. "Turn it off! They might see it!"

Jamie looked astonished, but he switched off the light, and held open the inside door for Patti. "What's up?" he asked.

Patti could see that Jamie and Pete had been putting together a complicated midnight snack—there were dirty dishes all over the counter under the glare of the kitchen light.

"Rustlers!" she told them, still puffing from her silent run up the drive. "Down by the woods. I think they can see the house lights from there!"

The boys stared at her.

"Damn!" said Jamie at last, his eyes blazing. "I'll phone the police."

But that only took a few minutes, and then there was nothing for them to do but wait. They paced around the kitchen, talking, feeling helpless.

"Dad's cattle!" Jamie said. He reached over and banged his hand on the kitchen table.

"We could turn off the kitchen light, so they think we've gone to bed," suggested Pete. "Then we can go out on the driveway and see if they come back up to the road."

"The policeman told me to keep everyone in the house," said Jamie. "He might phone back too."

"But we could watch the road from the back porch," Patti pointed out. "If our lights are out, they wouldn't see us from their truck. And we could hear the phone."

"True. And we could see which way they go, if they come up before the police get here. That'd be *something*, anyway."

They stood in the dark, listening to the familiar night sounds—the occasional sleepy squawk from the hen house, the crickets, an owl. They could almost believe it was an ordinary night.

"Look," whispered Jamie after a few minutes, "now you can just see the glow of a light over that rise in the field. They must have put some lights on."

"They didn't have *any* on when I passed them. And they're so quiet." said Patti. "I was afraid they would come up behind me while I was sneaking along the wagon track. And see me!"

"Whew!" exclaimed Jamie, looking worried. "Good point. Where are those police, anyway? They're not going to get here in time!"

"D'you suppose they're the same guys that've been rustling all over the neighbourhood?" said Pete.

"I *bet* they are," grumbled Jamie, angrily.

Patti was beginning to worry about Joan and Little Guy. Had they been heard? Were they in danger? Should she try to sneak back to check on them?

Just then the glow of the light from the bottom field went out. The three youngsters stood quietly, waiting. Soon they heard the approaching purr of a motor. They strained to see the truck through the dark.

"Look!" whispered Patti.

There it was—a dark shadow, poised for a moment on the edge of the road, then picking up speed in the direction away from the town.

"Wouldn't you know it!" exclaimed Jamie in disappointment, as, with a sudden grind of gears and a blaze of headlights, the truck disappeared around a bend in the road. "How are the police supposed to find them now?"

The sound of a siren answered him. They all ran down the driveway as flashing lights sped toward the farm and stopped beside the mailbox.

"They've just gone!" panted Jamie into the open window, pointing down the road.

"Right," said the officer at the wheel, waving them back from the car.

"Wait!" called a voice from beyond the car. "Wait!"

It was Joan. "I have the licence plate numbers," she gasped. "Both of them."

"Two trucks?" asked the second policeman, as he

wound down his window.

"No. Only one truck. Two licence plates—one on top of the other."

The policemen exchanged a glance.

"Let's have both of them," said the driver, a notebook and pen suddenly ready, while the other policeman reached for the radio microphone.

A minute later, they listened to the police siren scream off into the night. "How did you *get* the numbers?" Patti asked Joan in the silence it left behind.

"Well," explained Joan, "Little Guy had settled down, and I was worried about you. So I just crept up to the fence and walked carefully along it—staying among the trees, of course—till I saw them. There were only two men that I could see, and they were having trouble driving the cattle toward the truck—they kept breaking away, first one, then the other. They were still quite far away, so I squeezed through a hole in the fence and crawled under the loading ramp where I hoped they wouldn't see my flashlight. I just read the numbers, then ran back to the woods. When the truck headed up the field, I followed it."

The others were silent.

Joan shrugged. "I thought, if the police don't come in time, how would they know who they're looking for without a licence plate number?"

Jamie nodded. "With the number, they can find out who owns the truck and where he lives. But how did you know there were *two* plates?"

Joan shrugged again. "It was easy to see, up that close."

"But how did you *remember* two numbers?" asked Pete as they all walked back to the house."

"I don't know," confessed Joan. "I just did."

It was nearly one o'clock in the morning and they were still wide awake, making popcorn in the kitchen, when Mom and Dad came home. The police had phoned just an hour or so before. Jamie was to give Dad a message when he came home: he was to come to the address Jamie wrote down, about fifty miles away, to pick up the two stolen cattle. The police from that town, given Joan's information over the radio, had been parked and waiting for the thieves when they turned into their driveway.

Pete and Jamie went with Dad to hook the horse trailer up to the pickup.

"*Both* of them!" Dad kept saying, shaking his head as he headed out the door.

Mom took off her pretty dress and put on her jeans and running shoes to walk the girls back down to the camp and hear their whole story. Everything, from the beginning. She was quiet after that, as they walked along, and that made Patti nervous.

"You both took a big chance," she said at last. "Both of you. A big chance. I know you were being careful, but still … Especially you, Joan. It turned out well, but what if it hadn't?"

It was quiet again for a few moments as they all thought about it. The moon had finally come out, and they didn't even need their flashlights till they came to the wood.

"You took a chance too, Mrs. Blackburn," Joan said, tentatively. Then she stopped and looked at Mom, and Patti could see she was crying a little bit.

"You took a chance on me. A big chance. I think it's going to turn out okay too—but what if it hadn't?"

Mom looked at Patti, then Joan. Then she put her arms around both girls and gave them a big hug.

"Grug," said Patti, her voice muffled in Mom's sweater.

"What's *that*?" said Joan, wiping her eyes.

"Group hug," said Mom.

She turned them both toward the path again, and just then they heard a low whicker of welcome.

"I don't suppose you girls are nervous about staying here tonight," Mom said, only it was really a question.

"With Little Guy to look after us?" laughed Patti. But that wasn't really a question at all.

Pie Factory

The sun was down, and the lights were on in the house already. Patti crossed the road and started briskly up the driveway: she couldn't wait to talk to Mom and Dad. Just a few minutes ago, as they ate their soup and bannock supper down at the camp, Joan had told her something that bothered her. Really bugged her. What the heck was going on with Joan, anyway?

Right now, barn chores finished, Jamie was probably still out there, sanding the coffee table he was making for his scout camp badge. Dad and Mom were likely sitting in the living room. Dad would have his paper open, chuckling every now and then and reading out bits to Mom. And Mom …

Mom would be perched on a stool under the best lamp in the room, carving on Joan's house gnome—the one Jamie had started with the chainsaw, the day of the work-bee at the cabin. In fact, for the past two weeks she hadn't done any mending or knitting or ironing in the evenings. She hadn't played a game with Patti or even read a book—Mom, who loved reading!

By now, wood chips would have escaped the newspaper under the old table Dad had found for her carving, some of them even scattered over onto the good carpet. Patti shook her head about this. She could just imagine what Mom would say if she or Jamie decided to do some carving in the living room!

But it wasn't the wood chips that troubled her really: it was Joan and Mom. They had both changed somehow, and Patti needed to figure it out.

"Hi, honey!" said Mom cheerfully, peering at her over a pair of Dad's glasses.Patti did a double take. She had never seen Mom wearing glasses.

"What kind of day did you have?" Mom asked.

Dad lowered his paper to smile at Patti too.

"Okay," answered Patti vaguely, her face troubled. "Mom, how come Joan and I are going to make *pies* on Friday afternoon, instead of working on the cabin? She told me about it a few minutes ago."

Mom put her knife down and took off the glasses. "I suppose because Joan offered to do it to help me." She looked at Patti thoughtfully. "Because she knew I had to work at the bank till noon on Saturday, and the haying starts on Sunday, and I promised my usual fifteen pies for the crews' lunches. Also, she didn't want to give up the whole of Sunday to help serve the lunches—she would rather make pies on Friday afternoon." Mom was obviously puzzled. "Patti, you said *you'd* rather work on the cabin on Sunday too, rather than help with the haying this year. Remember?"

Patti nodded, uneasily. She knew Mom could use some help. It probably *was* a good idea to make the pies, but … She sighed. "It's just … well, it's one more day when we don't get on with the cabin. And that's happened so many times lately …"

"Are you worrying about all the time Joan spends with me in the garden these days?" asked Mom. She looked at Dad and laughed. "Well, there's certainly been a big change in Joan there—she can tell the difference now between a weed and an onion!

What's *really* bothering you, Patti?" She was serious again. "Maybe I should have asked you first about the pies. But, after all, you've helped me make those every summer since you were knee high to a grasshopper!"

"I suppose so." Patti sat on the arm of the couch and thought for a minute.

"Sometimes," she said at last, "it seems like I'm the only one these days who wants to finish the cabin. As if …

as if Joan is actually *looking* for excuses not to get on with it. The summer is already half over, and we haven't even finished the walls yet. Doesn't she want to get a chance to live in the cabin? What's the point?"

"Maybe the point isn't the obvious one," Dad suggested.

Patti looked at him, surprised.

"Why do *you* think we all decided the cabin was a good idea?" asked Mom.

"Because Joan didn't want to stay with us here in the house right after her Mom died—she wanted to be alone, remember? And she needed a safe place to live. And … and because it would be *fun*—something to take her mind off her troubles."

"Do you think it's worked?" Mom asked.

"Oh, yes!" exclaimed Patti. "Joan is like herself again and …"

Patti stopped there.

"Well," she said slowly, "no, she's not like she used to be, not really. She's … she's not exactly *happy* all the time; she still misses her family a lot. But she's more … more interested in *doing* things, I guess. And that's like she used to be."

"Wanting to learn new things, try new things? With other people?" Mom suggested.

Patti nodded.

"Like … learning how to garden? Make apple pies?"

Mom's eyes were teasing.

Patti nodded again, reluctantly. She darted an alarmed look at Dad, then back at Mom—she didn't like the way this conversation was going. "Does that mean we might never *finish* the cabin?"

"Why did *you* want to build the cabin, Patti?" Dad asked. "Was it just to help Joan?"

Patti was surprised again. She had never considered it quite like that before. "No, I guess not," she answered thoughtfully. "Mostly, because I like doing that sort of thing—projects, making things, learning how to do things."

"Like riding horses. Learning to drive-in-harness," Mom said.

"Or training a chicken to perch on your wrist like a falcon," added Dad with a chuckle.

Patti looked at one and then the other, a slow smile finally breaking through as she remembered her early adventures with Chicky. "But," she declared firmly, "I like to *finish* the things I start!"

Mom and Dad both laughed.

"But what about you guys?" persisted Patti. "Won't it be a waste of all your work if we don't finish the cabin?" She pointed at the gnome, glowing under the lamp. "You've been working on Joan's house gnome for weeks, Mom—what's the point if there isn't even going to be a *house*?"

"Patti," said Mom, astonished, "you can't think I've been doing this just for Joan!"

Patti was flabbergasted. Of course, that's exactly what she *had* been thinking. She turned, embarrassed, from Mom's questioning look and studied the gnome. He had changed since the last time she looked. The lines were more distinct, and there were smooth planes here and there. There were muscles, too, and a strength and power to his whole body. Everything about his face, from his neat pointed ears to the smile that had appeared through the bushy moustache and beard, had come alive. Why hadn't Patti noticed before?

She was beginning to understand what it was that was different about Mom these days.

"For years my carving tools have been tucked away, waiting for me to find time for them," Mom was explaining now. "Sometimes I wondered if that time would ever come. Then, all of a sudden, when this dear old gnome popped up, down at Joan's cabin, he seemed to be the perfect opportunity. Just what we both needed—Joan and I. Something special I could make for her cabin, and something *very* special for me."

Patti nodded—that made sense.

"So, you see," Mom added with a laugh, "this was basically something *I* wanted to do. And now I've started carving again, I hope I never stop!"

She picked up her knife, slid on Dad's glasses, and

turned to study the gnome. "Thank you, Joan," she added, with feeling. There was a long, long silence while Mom put down the knife again, and began to work on a corner of the carving with a piece of sandpaper. Patti watched.

"I guess it's sort of the same for me," she said at last. "Building the cabin was something I *really* wanted to do. Sometimes it seemed almost too exciting to be true," she sighed, regretfully.

Dad looked at her over his paper with a sympathetic smile.

"Don't worry that the cabin won't get finished, Patti," he said. "You must know that all summer, Jamie and I have been *dying* to get our hands on Joan's project. It's something *we* wanted to do, just like you. Just be patient, sweetie, and let everything work itself out. It will."

The room was quiet again as Mom reached for the knife again, and began to peel off thin shavings of sweet-smelling pine.

"What about a pie *factory*?" suggested Joan. She had already picked two boxes of early yellow apples that morning. Mom's bags of frozen piecrust dough had been thawing for hours and her instructions were spread out on the table—three pages of them.

"Good idea," agreed Patti, happily.

It was after lunch, and she had already showered away the barn smell from her morning's work at the stables. Now they had a big job ahead of them, and Patti liked big jobs.

"We could have an assembly line production," she suggested. "But we'll have to clear all Mom's canisters off the counters to make room."

"The mixer too?" asked Joan. "And this basket of letters and stuff?"

"Nothing but pie making allowed on any counter!" declared Patti.

Half an hour later, Mom's homey kitchen had been stripped down to bare bones, and the living room looked like a garage sale. Joan took over the table. She cut open lumps of dough to be sure their centres were properly thawed, then she found the rolling pin and the flour canister and unwrapped the packages of aluminum pie plates to spread along the counter.

Meanwhile, Patti clamped the apple peeler to the edge of the counter. She fetched the biggest mixing bowl from the summer kitchen, a bucket for the peelings and one box of apples. "Fifteen pies!" she exclaimed. "This might turn out to be as much fun as cabin-building!"

"We'll have to rush to get the first four pies into the oven," said Joan, who was re-reading the instructions.

"Everything has to be finished by five-thirty, so we can put your Mom's casserole in the oven for supper. But once we have that first four in, we have nearly an hour to get the next batch done, because that's how long they take to cook. I think we can just do it."

The summer kitchen screen door banged shut. Jamie stood in the doorway, looking around the main kitchen with his mouth open. He was covered in oil from work with the tractor, and he was wet with sweat.

"Apple pie factory," explained Patti, sparing him a quick glance. "Let's mix up four batches of apples at the same time, then," she said to Joan, as if there had been no interruption. "That'll save time."

"Sounds good," agreed Joan. She stopped her pastry rolling to rush to a drawer for measuring cups.

"Hey, what about my lunch?" protested Jamie. "You haven't left me any room in here!"

"Let's see—that'll be two cups of sugar," answered Patti, pushing aside some lumps of dough and pointing to a small corner of the table for Jamie.

"Where *is* the sugar?" asked Joan.

"Oops—the sugar went to the living room—it's in the biggest canister," said Patti, whirring her apple peeler at top speed. Coils of peelings fell into the bucket.

"Where the heck's the bread box, then?" complained Jamie, hands on his hips.

"In the living room too, I suppose," answered Patti

briskly. "Jamie!" She watched him stride angrily through the kitchen. "Don't forget to wash up!"

"So, are you the boss here now?" Jamie scowled at her, flattening himself against the doorjamb to make room for Joan and the sugar to pass.

"What's next?" asked Joan.

"Ah-h … cornstarch!" read Patti. The upstairs bathroom door slammed. "Uh … two tablespoons. Then half a teaspoon of salt. I'll mix it, if you like, Joan, while you get the first bottom pie crust ready."

"I'll do four bottoms first," said Joan, "then the tops after the filling is in."

"Oh, we mustn't forget to preheat the oven," exclaimed Patti, reaching for the stove.

All was quiet for a while, except for the thump of the rolling pin, the whirr of the apple peeler, and Patti's quiet murmur as she measured the sliced apples. Jamie went to the fridge to find his lunch makings, cut some bread, and his chair scraped the floor as he pulled it up to his corner of the table. Patti used the big spoon to mix all the ingredients together before she spooned it all evenly into the four pastry bottoms. She dotted them with little clumps of butter, then checked the kitchen clock. "We've gotta move faster!" she exclaimed. "Have you got the tops ready?"

"The trouble is these edges," said Joan a moment later. She had folded each top and cut the slashes according to Mom's instructions, then laid each one carefully over the apples. But how to fasten the two layers of pastry together? That's all the instructions said: "fasten".

Patti tried to push and pinch the edges together, but they definitely weren't "fastened". She looked at Joan in desperation.

"They'll leak all the insides out," she said. "It'll look awful."

"You put a bit of water along the edges," said Jamie, through a mouthful of sandwich, "and then you *twist* them."

"What?" The girls looked at him in surprise.

"Like this." Jamie pushed back his chair, wiping his hands on his dirty jeans. He reached for the first pie.

Patti opened her mouth to protest—then she closed it again. She watched in amazement as Jamie first wetted a finger under the tap, then ran it along each pastry edge to act as a sort of glue. Then he closed a finger and thumb of both hands over the two edges of the pastry and twisted them in opposite directions. He turned the pie again and again and repeated the operation. In a matter of moments, the pie looked just like one of Mom's.

"How did …?" Patti was speechless.

"Some of us just pay attention to things," said Jamie smugly.

Just as Joan finished the other pies under his watchful eye, the phone rang. "Hi, Mom," answered Patti airily, peering into the kitchen from the hallway. She signalled madly to Joan, pointing from the pies to the oven.

"Sure, Mom, the first lot is in. Is it really two o'clock already? Yep, we'll watch the tops carefully."

Suddenly she made a strange hissing sound. Joan looked up from shutting the oven door. Patti's hand was over the mouthpiece, and this time she was signalling in the opposite direction—from the stove and back to the counter. "Cinnamon?" she was saying to Mom, calmly. "Of course!" But her eyes were wide with horror as she mouthed the message to Joan: *take them out.*

"Gotta go, Mom, or we'll get behind. Bye!"

"Cinnamon!" she wailed as she put down the phone. "How could we forget the cinnamon?"

It turned out to be much harder to take a top crust off than to put it on—especially when it was properly "fastened". A long time later the first four pies were in the oven again. But how could they possibly finish them all in time now? What could they do about that casserole for supper? The girls were in despair.

Jamie licked his fingers after he popped the last of his apple turnover into his mouth.

"How many pies?" he asked calmly.

"Fifteen!" chorused the girls.

"Let's see …" Jamie did some quick calculations on his fingers. "That'll be seven-thirty at least. Too late. I'll take the casserole over to Pete's on my bike—his folks are in town, so I can use their oven. I was going there now anyway. I'll bring it back at supper time."

He turned at the door, after the casserole had been wrapped snugly in tea towels.

"Don't forget to hire *me* when you set up your pie factory," he said with a smirk.

"Gr-r-r ..." said Patti, grinding her teeth.

Joan nodded her agreement. "But I think we know now—building log cabins is more fun, and a *lot* easier, than making pies," she said.

Solutions

Why did I *say* anything, anyway? Patti scolded herself furiously as she bicycled home from the stables. Sometimes she wished she could just keep her mouth shut, instead of always leaping into things, trying to solve problems.

On the other hand ...

She sighed. Mr. Anderson was a good friend. He had done so much for her and Little Guy. And he was the one who *taught* them to drive-in-harness in the first place. She supposed she owed him all the help she could give him.

From the beginning she had loved his idea of a trail ride campout for all the young people at the stables. So did everyone else. It had, in fact, become the most looked-forward-to event of the whole summer, outshining even the usual preparations for the Fall Fair Horse Show.

Mr. Anderson was so chatty and friendly that he had managed to get a lot of influential people in the community behind the project, too. He had already established a winding wagon trail linking several of their fields and woodlots.

"You won't believe the place I've found for our destination camping spot!" he had reported to the campout group, his face flushed with excitement. "Imagine this, everyone: a green meadow that borders the river at its widest turn. Shade trees and a firm, flat pasture area for riding and tethering the horses. A safe beach for swimming. And it's only twenty miles from Carolyn's stables! Most amazing of all, Mr. Wardly, the farmer who owns it, is absolutely delighted that we chose *him* to ask!"

"Well!" Carolyn had beamed. "Terrific! It's been my dream for years—setting up something like this. Thank you, Mr. Anderson!"

Wild applause, punctuated by a few shrill whistles.

It had all begun in the first days of the summer when Mr. Anderson arranged to borrow Little Guy every two weeks to teach several of Carolyn's students how to handle the driving reins and the whip. Soon, four of them, including Patti's friend Nancy, had acquired either wagons or buggies and harnesses of their own, and had begun to teach their horses under Mr. Anderson's watchful eye. As enthusiasm grew, Mr. Anderson had hatched the idea of the trail-ride campout at the end of the summer to celebrate the beginning of a harness club, and the recent purchase of his own horse and buggy. Feeling expansive, he had then invited Carolyn, and anyone else at the stables who was interested, to come along, riding their horses.

"With three wagons and three buggies," he had pointed out, "we can carry the camping equipment of all the horse riders. The more the merrier!"

But by today's meeting, it had become obvious that Mr. Anderson's jovial generosity had led him, and the whole project, into a tight spot. With only a week to go now till the campout, he had successfully tied up all the loose ends, except for one important one: the provisioning and cooking of the meals for eighteen people on the five-day trail ride.

"I should have paid more attention to this problem," he had confessed, that morning, to a tack room of very solemn faces. "Somehow, I just assumed that a kind mother or two would help us with the catering. Cooking isn't my department, I guess, or I would have taken it more seriously from the first."

He shook his head, sadly. "I'm sorry. I just didn't realize what a busy group of people your mothers are. I know they would help if they could …" He sighed and ran a hand through his curly white hair. "If someone could come up with a suggestion at this point, I'm sure we'd all be most grateful."

It had been a gloomy meeting. As Patti looked around at her friends, and Carolyn and Mr. Anderson, she was alarmed. But she was also puzzled. Why was this such a problem? All summer she had watched Joan try recipe after recipe on her campfire. It couldn't be *that* hard, could it? True, she had discussed the recipes with Mom, before and after—she had lots of help there. But the suppers Joan served Patti every evening were almost always delicious. How Patti wished, now, that she herself had paid more attention to Joan's cooking, instead of having her mind so stuck on the cabin project. Was it too late to learn? Surely they wouldn't have to give up the campout just because of the *cooking*!

"At Guide Camp," she had explained to the group, "we camp in groups of six. We plan our meals ahead of time and decide exactly what we have to bring. It's all pretty simple cooking—but it's okay. We don't starve or anything. And it's fun. Couldn't we do something like that?"

Mr. Anderson''s face had brightened with sudden hope. "Perhaps," he suggested, "we could find at least one mother in each group who would supervise the planning. Do you think?"

"I don't want to be a wet blanket," Carolyn had intervened, her face grim. "I think that's a terrific idea of Patti's. But, don't forget, at a Guide Camp there are always experienced leaders to help the girls with their food planning and cooking, and the details of the campfire and tents and so on."

"We do have the camping supervision part covered," put in Mr. Anderson. "I've had some experience there, myself. Also, I've asked Patti's brother Jamie to come along as an extra man. He's fourteen, now, and a veteran Scout camper."

Carolyn was still unconvinced. "I suspect provisioning and campfire cooking look a lot easier than they really are," she had said. "It isn't a matter of starving, Patti—but of safety and comfort. And fun. I'm perfectly happy to take charge of horse matters—but not cooking. Not for so many people."

At this, Mr. Anderson's face had fallen again. He had already asked every possible person in the neighbourhood.

Patti couldn't stand it any longer. "This summer," she had blurted out, "I've eaten a supper cooked over a campfire almost every night!" Then she had explained to everyone about Joan's summer. "I'm sure I could get Joan and Mom to help me make a menu, then a list of provisions for each group of six. Then, if they taught me how to cook all the meals during the week …" Her voice had begun to falter at this point.

"What we *need*," Carolyn had said, a determined spark in her eye, "is Joan herself. If she camped with us, she could teach us all. And your Mom, Patti—do you think she would help Joan with the planning?"

On the edge of their seats by then, the others were nodding hopeful agreement. Had a solution been found?

"I don't think ... I ..." Patti was dumbfounded at this sudden turn of events.

"I don't know," she had said, reluctantly. "I'll have to ask."

If only, Patti thought now, riding her bicycle home, she hadn't been so quick with her solutions. Because the truth was, she didn't *want* Joan to come on this camping trip.

All through the rest of the meeting that morning, visions of Joan's last weeks in school had flooded Patti's mind. Joan's chip on the shoulder. Her awful clothes. Her complete disregard of what anyone else thought. Patti was horrified and depressed at the thought of returning to those troubled times. To being stuck in the middle, between two sides, helpless to explain them to each other.

Joan had settled into Patti's family, now. Somehow, the cabin-building project had transformed an uncomfortable situation into a happy one. Joan was just *fine* as Patti's friend. And fine as a member of her family. But Joan at a campout? With all those other kids?

No. Absolutely not. It was one thing to have Jamie along—he knew most of her friends and was well liked. Jamie was okay. But Joan would be a disaster.

I'll learn the cooking, Patti resolved. It was the only

answer. There wasn't nearly enough time, she knew, but she could do it if she really tried. She *would* do it!

"What a good idea!" Mom interrupted Patti's account of the dilemma of the campout group right at the point where Carolyn had suggested Joan should come along too.

"But …" Patti said, dismayed. She hadn't even explained *her* idea yet!

"Dad and I have been worrying about Joan lately," interrupted Mom again. "It's high time she moved out a bit from our family. Why, only three weeks from now, she'll be with Aunt Kate in the city, facing a completely new home and neighbourhood and school. She needs to widen her scope and get back some of her confidence."

"But …" Patti protested again.

Once more Mom interrupted, excited. "It's an excellent solution for the trail-ride campout, isn't it? Joan has learned a lot about cooking this summer. She's quite capable of taking charge. And what a perfect opportunity for Joan herself! Now, I just need to focus some time on the planning with her."

Before Patti knew what was happening, she was on

her way to summon Joan for a conference up at the house.

Patti's hopes began to lift once the situation had been explained to Joan.

"No, please no!" Joan looked with panic from Mom to Dad. "I can't possibly!" she said, pleading. "I'm running out of time, can't you see? I have to work on the cabin."

Maybe they would listen to Patti's idea now!

But Joan's objections didn't last for five minutes against arguments and reasons. Patti couldn't help thinking Mom and Dad were unusually pushy about this whole affair.

"The cabin walls have been finished for two weeks, now," Dad pointed out, logically. "Patti herself wouldn't be happy about going on the campout—she said so just the other day—except that you two have almost finished with peeling the top beams and ridge pole. Didn't you say you have the thin poles ready, too? The supports for the tin roof?"

Both Patti and Joan nodded, reluctantly.

"In fact," Mom said, "you're as good as ready right now for the 'raise the roof' work-bee the Saturday after the campout, aren't you?" Both girls nodded again.

"Besides, the campout *needs* you, doesn't it?" She was looking at Joan, with that 'Mom look' that Patti knew so well. "They *need* both you and me. Maybe we can pull things together for them?"

Joan nodded, resigned and thoughtful. It would be

impossible for her to say no to something Mom really wanted, Patti thought in despair.

"Let's see," said Mom, reaching for pencil and paper, "five days means fifteen meals. What about ... well, spaghetti sauce, made ahead of time and frozen for the first night? And pancakes, of course."

"The mix for those could be made up ahead of time, too," Joan suggested, slowly. She was beginning to look interested.

Patti listened, absently, as they briefly discussed the ins and outs of stew, corn chowder, and bannock. Once again, she was imagining Joan among all her horse-riding friends. She shuddered inwardly. Maybe ... maybe *she* should stay home herself, Patti thought. They didn't need *her*!

Suddenly she caught Dad's eye. It was a much fiercer, sterner eye than usual. As if he had been reading her mind. Patti could feel the beginning of a flush.

"How will Joan travel on the trail ride?" Jamie was asking. He hadn't said a thing till now.

Patti was glad of the interruption. "Why, on the wagon, I suppose," Mom said, surprised. "Is there ...?"

"It's just that Patti and I will be on the seat," he pointed out, "and if we're carrying tents and things ..."

Here was an objection Patti hadn't even thought of!

Then she remembered. "I promised Sylvia today," she told them all, reluctantly, "that I'd ride her pony on the trail ride, since Jamie will be there to drive the wagon. Her family is going to the lake for their summer vacation, and she hates for Bets to miss any fun."

I *can't* skip the trail ride, after all, Patti thought. I've promised. Last summer, Sylvia had loaned Bets to Patti so she could learn to ride when Little Guy was still too lame. She owed them both this favour. She was stuck.

"So there *is* a place for Joan, after all," said Mom, looking relieved.

And that was that.

The next afternoon, Patti walked slowly down the path toward Joan's camp. She didn't want to, but she *always* turned up at the camp in the afternoons after her morning at the stables—how would she explain it if she didn't? Besides, Mom had phoned from the bank with a message for her to pass on to Joan.

Patti and Joan hadn't been alone together since last night. The rest of her family was pleased with the new plans, and this morning, at the stables, everyone in the campout group had been jubilant. But Patti was smouldering—with anxiety and resentment.

Because of that, she dreaded the things that might get

said. Not by Joan—*she* seemed to have accepted Mom's and Dad's decision, though Patti knew she wasn't entirely happy about it. No, it was what she herself might say that worried Patti. After all, the last time she felt like this, Joan had ended up running away! Who knew what kind of disaster another angry outburst could cause?

Patti felt trapped. A person could get angry about being afraid to get angry!

Chop! Chop!

"What're you *doing*?" Patti was startled by the shadowy figure in the woods beside the path. Her voice was sharp.

But Joan's eyes sparkled with that particular look she had when she was wielding her hatchet. "Getting some green, whippy saplings," she said, puffing a bit from her exertions.

"What for?"

"We're going to turn the wagon into an old-fashioned covered wagon," said Joan. "We're going to be pioneers! Going west!"

"How?" Patti was puzzled as she looked at the stack of thin, green saplings on the ground.

"Jamie showed me how to put a green stick in the fire to heat it, then bend it around a thick tree trunk," Joan explained. "That makes the hoops. He's going to find some old pieces of pipe and attach them to the side of the wagon for the ends of the hoops to fit into. We're going to use the old tarp over my cooking shelter for the wagon cover."

"Oh, yeah," Patti said, slowly. "I remember reading about that when we were building the model cabin. Are we making it right now?" she asked hopefully. A new project might get her through the afternoon …

"Yep," said Joan, hacking off the branches from the sapling she was holding. "I've almost got enough. D'ya want to build up the fire for me?"

Patti blew on the ashes, her hand busy with kindling and her thoughts calmer already. I'd rather be *doing* something than be angry, she thought.

Besides … "Wait till the others see *our* wagon," she declared, as Joan dragged her saplings into the camp clearing. Something like this might just make a difference to how the others thought about Joan.

But Joan shrugged, indifferent. "Who cares?" she said. "Anyway, Jamie is going to sleep in the tent, so he can be with Mr. Anderson and the other boys. It'll be you and me sleeping in the covered wagon. We can park it *way* away from everyone else!"

Patti opened her mouth to protest.

Joan looked at her, suddenly fierce. "I've promised your mom I'll show people how to cook," she said. "Just because they can't find anyone else. But that's *all* I promised."

Patti glared at Joan, who was glaring back at her. She

bit her lip. Then she remembered Mom's message. She took a deep breath. "Mom's found a sweatshirt and jeans in town—she phoned me just now. She wants you to be ready to go with her tomorrow morning to try them on."

"Your mom's *good* at blackmail," Joan said, whacking at her green saplings. "Either we buy my school things now, or I have to do it with Aunt Kate later. And Aunt Kate might not really have time …" Joan laughed, a little bitterly. She shrugged. "Might as well do it now."

"I guess she wants you to have some nice things for the trail ride," said Patti, carefully. This was something to be thankful for, anyway—Mom had paid *some* attention to Patti's worry about Joan's raggedy clothes.

"Oh well," observed Joan, "no harm in packing them, is there? There's nothing to say I have to *wear* them." She hacked industriously at a knot on one of the sticks. "If they *want* me," she said, with a glint in her eye, "they'll have to take me just the way I am!"

A Proper Cook

Little Guy was in his horse trailer, which was hooked up to the pickup; right behind the trailer rumbled the wagon, the hoops and covers carefully packed inside.

"We look like a train," Patti commented to Dad, as she craned her neck out the window of the pickup. "Going a whole fifteen miles an hour."

"Well, it's a good thing we're so early, and there's no one else on the road," he said, glancing anxiously at the rear-view mirror.

Patti could see Jamie and Joan in the back of the pick-up, perched on tents and packs and boxes of food. Joan's long black hair was getting tangled in the wind, and one knee stuck out through a hole in her oldest jeans. Worst of all, she was wearing the red shirt—the one she used for her dirtiest work on the cabin. Mom had made no comment, and the look she gave Patti made sure she didn't either.

Once again, Patti checked to see that the fishing rods were still safely stowed at Jamie's feet. It was strange how important her fishing gear had become for this trip. She had never thought of herself as especially keen on fishing—not like Jamie, anyway. But today she took comfort in imagining herself all alone on a peaceful riverbank, well away from the main camp. And from Joan. It might turn out to be the escape she needed.

"I'm glad the trail ride begins right at Carolyn's," said Dad. "I don't think I'd be doing this if it was a longer drive."

But Patti was wishing that the drive *would* take forever. She didn't like the dread feeling in the pit of her stomach. At school, she thought, the other kids at least *knew* Joan and her, and that had been bad enough—but many of Patti's riding friends were new, and her acceptance there had been hard won over the past year. What would they think once they met *Joan*?

Soon they were making their way slowly down Carolyn's bumpy driveway. "Holy smokes!" exclaimed Dad as they came around a bend to a scene of complete confusion. There were cars parked in every possible space, and parents and kids carrying loads to the two wagons and two buggies in the pasture next to the stables. He pulled up as far from the commotion as he could.

"You go ahead, Patti, and get Bets ready," he said. "I'll unload the pickup, and help load the wagon."

"Hi Patti!" It was Jenny, beside the pickup before it had even stopped completely. "I've got a pony to ride!" she shrieked joyfully. "Can you believe it? Carolyn finally got hold of Shadow's owner yesterday. I can *come!*"

Patti forgot her worries for the moment as she slipped down from the front seat.

"Fantastic!" she said. "Mary and Eric are all set too!" Everyone knew that Carolyn had been determined to find a horse for each of the three stable workers who worked with Patti.

"Is this Joan?" asked Jenny, her long blonde braids fairly bouncing with her exuberance."Uh … yep!" answered Patti uneasily.

She watched Joan jump out of the pickup and head to the wagon without even glancing back at Jenny, although she must have heard the question.

"I think she's worried about the stuff in the wagon," Patti explained, but Jenny seemed to have ignored the snub.

"I'll go back now and say hi to her," Jenny said.

Just then, Jamie appeared around the pickup. He had heard everything too. "I'm on my way to help Joan get Little Guy and hitch him up," he said. "You're Jenny, aren't you? I'm Jamie. C'mon and I'll introduce you to Joan. We're going to put the covers on the wagon, too. Want to help?"

"I've gotta go," said Patti desperately to Dad, who was on his way back to the pickup. "I've got to get Bets ready."

He nodded and waved her away, and she blew him a kiss.

"Thanks!" she called.

And then she was running, gratefully, in the opposite direction.

"Did your group get all the food on the list?"

"Yeah. Two of our moms did the shopping on Saturday. Then we all got together to cook the spaghetti sauce at my house yesterday. We put together the mixes too—the pancakes and bannock. How about you?"

Patti stopped buckling Bets' girth for a moment to listen to the conversation outside her stall. She didn't recognize the voices.

"Oh, we forgot a couple of things, naturally—phone calls all over the place last night. But I think we've got it together now."

"Have you met Joan yet?"

"Not yet. But I hear she's a regular old grouch. Snaps your head off!"

"I'm in big trouble, then," the second voice said. "I can't even boil an egg properly."

Patti stood quietly beside Bets. She would wait till they had gone before she led the pony out.

"Looks like Joan's going to be a real, proper camp cook, then, eh? Cranky and crabby like they're supposed to be!" laughed a third voice. Patti *did* know that voice—it was her friend Nancy.

"She's got a proper old-fashioned covered wagon too," Nancy continued. "Have you guys seen it yet? It's a chuck wagon—just like a real cook on a western wagon train!"

"Really? How …"

The voices faded as the *clip, clop* of hooves on the cement stable floor turned into the soft thump of feet on the paddock sawdust. Patti remembered that Nancy already knew Joan—last summer, when Nancy came to the farm often to help Patti and Little Guy get ready for the Fall Fair Show, Joan was sometimes there as well. They liked each other, too. But then Nancy got along with everyone.

"Jamie and Joan can manage the wagon without us," Patti whispered to Bets as she led her from the stall. "Let's go and find us a place near the front of the line-up."

Patti had taken longer than she realized in the barn. There was a definite line of wagons and buggies in the driveway now, with Mr. Anderson in the lead, looking jovial and chatty and eager to start. Little Guy, harnessed to his covered wagon, was at the end of the line, back almost as far as the main road. Although all the gear and provisions had already been divided among the buggies, a group of chattering people still crowded around his wagon. Patti didn't want to know what was happening there. Instead, she looked ahead to the open gate that led along a beaten path across Carolyn's pasture to the beginning of their trail. It was a sunny day, with a windy, August feel to the air. A perfect day for an adventure. Firmly she turned Bets toward Carolyn and the horse riders, waiting impatiently in the lane.

Time flew as they wound their way slowly along wagon roads through woodlots and over fields. The riders looked for straight, open places for some good canters, but then they always circled back to the more sober procession of wagons and buggies.

"Gotta keep an eye on all that food!" was the motto they tossed back and forth.

It was noon before they knew it, and they had arrived at their lunch spot, about seven miles along the trail. Circling the wagons on a hill overlooking the river, they gave their horses the hay they had brought, then made a bucket brigade to the river to bring up their water. Then they sat in a large, cheerful group with their lunch kits, talking about all the things they had brought and the things they had forgotten.

Joan sat with a group of girls that included Jenny and Nancy; she was eating and listening to the jokes and laughter. Jamie sat with Mr. Anderson, deep in conversation about something. Patti watched them all from a place higher on the hill next to Bets, who was munching noisily, drowning out the talk from below. It was peaceful, if a bit lonely, up there, looking down on the party. But today, Patti decided 'a bit lonely' was just what she needed.

The camping site, when they arrived at mid-afternoon, was as lovely as Mr. Anderson had promised: a strip of birch and maple woods next to the river, with a large open field beside it. There was not a house or farm in sight.

Once everyone had spread out and chosen their camping spots, and the horses had been unhitched, unsaddled, and tethered out in the middle of the field, Mr. Anderson called a meeting.

"What's first?" he asked Jamie.

"Horses, of course," put in Carolyn. "Always horses! Let's do the bucket brigade again, and then I want to do a check on them all before we start on the camping stuff."

"Latrines after that," said Jamie, looking very businesslike and grown up. Patti noticed how deep his voice was getting. How come she hadn't noticed that before? "I think only two people from each group are needed to do that. Bring your shovel and tarp, and we'll find ourselves a place in that little wood over there, well away from the river. Meanwhile, the others could unload the wagons and choose a tent site."

"Tent pitching after that?" Mr. Anderson looked around and everyone nodded in agreement. "Then fireplaces?" he looked at Joan questioningly.

"Nope," said Joan, bluntly. Patti sucked in her breath anxiously; Joan wasn't even smiling when she said that. How rude it sounded! "We need wood first. No point in fireplaces without the wood for a fire!" Joan explained.

Mr. Anderson laughed good-naturedly. "Good point," he said, and Patti slowly let out her breath.

Later, it was Patti alone who combed the woods for kindling and larger branches, while the others were busy putting up tents under Jamie's supervision. She stacked the firewood in a pile near the path, then headed back for more. "*Our* beds are all set in the wagon," she had said to Joan before she left.

She was finding it hard to look right at her when she said this. The anger was back again, like something in her chest that made it hard to talk.

"I'm going to collect *all* the firewood for our group," she had explained carefully, looking at her shoes, "while you organize the food and the fireplace. I'll stack it all right over there by the path. I'll collect some extra too, in case one of the groups doesn't get enough to *suit* you."

Did that sound sarcastic?

Quickly she continued, "And I'll feed Little Guy and Bets. But *then* I'm going fishing until suppertime."

She and Joan had exchanged a brief guarded look, before each turned away to her job.

Patti was relieved to be away from the camp, from all the excited talk and laughter. She was especially glad to know she would be fishing while Joan was supervising the building of the fireplaces. She shuddered at the thought of all the impossible things Joan might say!

But she wasn't entirely glad. Patti stopped for a moment to look into the cool woods and think about it. She was sad, too, she realized. Maybe even more sorry than angry. She and Joan had become good friends over the summer, in a way they hadn't been before. They had worked together and shared so much. Patti had thought they would always be friends, and help each other—yet she had left Joan to deal with all those strangers by herself.

Well, she rationalized, as she dropped the last armload of wood on the pile, a fish or two would be a contribution, wouldn't it? A kind of gift. Besides, she couldn't think of any other way she could … Suddenly, Patti put her hands to her face in dismay—she had just remembered about suppertime, when Joan would show everyone how to make the bannock!

It was cooler already on the riverbank, and the sun had long since disappeared behind the trees. Patti checked her watch. Almost six o'clock. But she didn't need her watch to tell her it was time to go back to camp—for the past half hour she had smelled whiffs of campfire smoke. She had known the exact point in the afternoon when the tents and fireplaces and wood chores were finished. From around the bend in the river she had heard Jamie's voice, then the answers of one or two other boys. She also knew how many fish they caught. Ten minutes ago, those voices had wandered back to camp.

With a sigh, Patti wrapped her one reasonable-sized trout in a few big maple leaves. She had already cleaned it with her pocketknife—without Jamie's help, too. At least she had something to show for her afternoon. She had missed the agreed-upon meeting time for dinner preparation, and she knew she had missed it on purpose.

A burst of laughter surprised Patti as she neared her group's campsite. She stopped and peered around a tree. There was a crowd around Joan's campfire. Everyone's there, thought Patti. All she could see was a cluster of backs.

Another burst of laughter. Then another. What on earth was going on?

No one noticed her approach. She tucked her fishing rod under the wagon and looked for a place to join the others.

"Yay! She did it!"

There were sudden shouts, clapping, and stamping. Patti reached the edges of the crowd just as it shifted, and there, beside the fire ring, were Joan and Nancy. Joan was laughing helplessly along with everyone else. Nancy was squatting, a frying pan in her hand and a comical expression on her face.

"What's she doing?" Patti was next to Eric.

"She's flipped her bannock once," he said, without taking his eyes off Nancy. "Like a pancake. Right up in the air. Then she caught it! Now she's going to do it again."

"If you drop it, that's *your* dinner!" someone called from the crowd.

"Good point!" said Nancy, as if the thought had never occurred to her. She made her usual clown face, complete with crossed eyes, and changed her mind on the spot. Everyone laughed again.

"So what's next, Cookie?" she asked Joan cheekily.

Joan waved them all away. "That's it," she said. "You've all got your spaghetti water almost boiling. Just be sure to keep stirring the sauce, or you'll burn it. Like I did the first time."

The group melted away, everyone chatting and joking. Patti was left standing alone with Joan.

"I only caught one," she said, shyly holding out the fish in its bed of leaves.

Joan nodded, still smiling. "We'll cook it after we've done the bannock, okay?"

The two girls stood and grinned at one another for a moment, while the people in their group clustered around the stores boxes with their pots and pans.

"Tomorrow we get to swim," said Patti. "I hope you remembered your swimsuit."

It was almost dark now, and Patti and Joan were inside their covered wagon with their flashlights. Patti was looking through her pack for her favourite sweatshirt; she was getting ready to join the group that was beginning to gather around Mr. Anderson's campfire.

"I don't *have* a swimsuit," confessed Joan as she unrolled her sleeping bag. "My shorts and t-shirt will have to do."

Patti stopped her rummaging for a moment to stare at Joan. Was this *another* problem? Just when things were going well? Then she had a new thought: why did it matter? If Joan was okay with it, why should it bother *her*?

"Good idea," she said at last.

Why not, after all? She ran her fingers through her hair to smooth it after pulling her sweatshirt on. And then she had another thought. Should I ask her, she wondered.

She hesitated. "Are you coming to the campfire?" she said at last. "Mr. Anderson is going to play his guitar."

"Maybe ... in a while," answered Joan, pulling pyjamas out of her pack.

Will she come? Patti worried about *that* for a moment as she slipped down off the wagon. Will the others notice if she doesn't, and think she's weird?

And then that great idea came back to her: why should anyone care, as long as she does what she wants?

Patti drew a deep breath. She liked this new way of looking at things. Joan was just Joan—why should she *have* to fit in? Besides, Patti had to admit, Joan seemed to be doing very well so far without any help from her.

They were in the middle of "She'll Be Comin' Round the Mountain," when Patti spotted Joan slip through the dusk like a shadow and settle on a log close to Mr. Anderson. Leaning forward to get a better view, Patti saw that Joan's long hair had been brushed back into a ponytail, and she was wearing the new black jeans and grey-green sweatshirt that Mom had picked out for her.

She looked older all of a sudden, and a little bit shy. Of course, thought Patti, she probably doesn't know any of these songs—she's probably never been to a camp before.

"She'll be wearing pink pyjamas when she comes …"

Joan wasn't singing along with the others, or even trying to. She seemed, in fact, to have suddenly forgotten everyone else. She was watching, fascinated, as Mr. Anderson's fingers worked up and down the frets of the guitar, moving swiftly from one chord to the next.

Everybody's Project

"Excuse me, sir," said Patti. She bobbed her head respectfully in the direction of the gnome, then shifted her hold on the piece of galvanized roofing to manoeuvre it over the gnome to Jamie's ladder. Joan was holding the other side.

"So *sorry* to keep bothering you," said Joan, as she passed the gnome.

Mom laughed. She was sorting the sheets of old roofing to find the right lengths.

"You'll turn his head if you treat him like royalty," she said.

"*They* can't turn his head," said Jamie from the top of his ladder. "But *I* could. Just let me at that chainsaw again, and I'll have his head right off in no time!"

Jamie's job was to catch hold of the end of each metal sheet that the girls brought him, then pull it up so it was lined up against the previous one on the roof. Next, he helped the girls to slide it up to Dad, who was perched on the centre roof beam. Jamie then nailed down his end of it to the strapping boards as far up as he could reach, while Dad hammered down the top half.

The gnome, perched on Joan's special wood chopping block beside the cabin path, watched them all come and go with an expression of benign indifference. His wise eyes seemed to be focussed on much more serious matters.

"He's all yours, now, Joan," Mom had said the night before. "You can take your gnome with you when Aunt Kate comes to get you tomorrow."

They were having their final dinner together, up at the house, and talking about the next day, which would be their last work-bee on the cabin. And Joan's last day with them on the farm, till she came back in a few weeks for Thanksgiving.

"Oh!" Joan had looked at Mom, her brown eyes wide with surprise. "I don't know …" she said thoughtfully. "Don't you think he *really* belongs down at the cabin? I'd like it better if I knew he was there, looking after things till I come back." She had paused for a few moments, thinking. "Even if I only come sometimes, the cabin is my *real* home now." And then she looked around at each of them to see how they would react.

There had been another quiet moment at the dinner table then, as everyone considered the importance of what she had said. Then, one after another, they smiled and nodded yes. It sounded like absolutely the right decision.

"It's finished!"

It was almost lunchtime when the last piece of metal roofing had been hammered into place. After Dad and Jamie had taken down the ladders, they all stood looking at the cabin.

They didn't seem to have much to say.

"It doesn't seem quite so spanking new with that old roofing on top, does it?" said Mom finally.

That's exactly what Patti had been thinking. She looked at Joan.

"It's okay," said Joan, cautiously. "We don't want it to look *really* new, do we? It's supposed to be an old-time cabin, after all."

"I think you'll find that six months of rain and wind and snow will make it look like it belongs," said Dad reassuringly. "Let's see what it looks like inside."

They trooped into the tiny house. The floor gleamed with its light brown paint job, the log walls had been oiled, and the old door and window had been sanded and repainted. The two girls had even learned how to replace the two missing windowpanes. This morning the cabin had looked and smelled so clean and new, but now, when they looked up … How disappointing, thought Patti. The old roofing looked even more battered and grubby than she had feared it would.

"It does look bad, I agree," said Dad. "But I've been thinking lately anyway, it might be a pity to leave the roof open like this on the inside—if we put up a proper ceiling, it would not only look better, but it could be insulated, and be a much warmer little cabin. I saw a pile of scrap lumber at the mill the other day—I'm sure if I sorted through it, I would find enough to cover such a small area. It would *look* better, but more important, that would allow us to stuff the insulation between the ceiling and the roof …" He pointed up to the spaces between the rafters.

"It's okay the way it is, you know," said Joan. "That sounds like a lot more work for you—I don't think …"

"Ah well," interrupted Dad, grinning at her, "that ceiling would keep it *so* much warmer in winter. Not much point in a *heating stove*, if there's no insulation, is there?"

"A stove?" exclaimed Patti and Joan together. Dad had insisted from the start that the cabin would be too small for a fireplace or a stove—it would have to be a summer cabin only, with a cooking shelter outside.

"Well," said Dad, "I've changed my mind. Mom and I were talking about it the other day, and Jamie reminded us that we have Gramma's little wood heater still, behind a pile of stuff in the workshop. It just needs oiling and it would tuck perfectly in here." He pointed to the corner near the front door. "These little stoves with their stove pipes are so much safer than fireplaces. And you girls have had a whole summer of practising fire safety, haven't you? It would mean you could spend some time down here even in the winter." There was a shine in his eyes, "Besides, you might not have noticed, but I'm having a great time with this little project. Wouldn't it be wonderful to finish it off properly before the snow flies?"

Mom laughed at him. "I think we've all noticed that we don't have to drag you down here to work on this project!"

Jamie had been thinking while they talked. "Joan," he said, "when I have the bunks built, and the stove is in and everything … um … do you think maybe Pete and I … um … could maybe, sometimes, on a weekend when you aren't here …"

Joan looked hard at Jamie, and then at Mom, suddenly worried.

"Will this … will this still be *my* home after I go?" she asked. "You guys will all have put so much work into it—like the furniture and the ceiling and the stove. Will the cabin still be *mine*?"

Mom put her hands on Joan's shoulders and pulled her closer.

"Joan," she said, looking earnestly into her troubled face, "this will *always* be your home, just like we agreed last night. Nothing will change that. Whatever we do on the cabin will be with your permission. And that includes if and how we use it when you aren't here." She darted a meaningful glance in Jamie's direction.

Joan looked back at Mom for a long moment, then nodded slowly. Then she smiled—a wide smile that lit up her face completely. Patti thought she had never seen Joan smile quite like that before.

"What I'd like," Joan said, "is for you all to finish the cabin if you want to, just the way we've talked about. Patti can describe it in detail when we talk on the phone—and I can sit in the apartment in the city and imagine it all and send along my orders and permission!" She turned to Jamie. "Sure," she said grandly, "you and Pete can stay here, as long as you leave it tidy. And keep the firewood covered and dry. Refill the water buckets. Sweep the floor. And wash the dishes. And the window. And the ceiling. And …"

She was laughing now, and so were Mom and Dad, as Jamie's head bowed lower and lower beneath each imaginary blow.

But Patti had stopped listening. She had some new ideas herself.

"A sleigh," she announced. "That's what we'll need when the snow comes. Do you suppose Maynard could find one, like he found the wagon?"

"A sleigh?" asked Dad.

"Yep. A sleigh. For Little Guy. So we can bring him down here in the snow when we can't use the wagon."

"Hey!" exclaimed Jamie. "This could be our maple syrup cabin in the spring. Perfect! The trees are right around here, after all, and ..."

He stopped suddenly as he saw all eyes turn to Joan. Sheepishly, he raised his eyebrows in question.

"Not without me, you won't!" Joan declared. "I've never made maple syrup—I'll absolutely *have* to come for that."

"We could build a huge bonfire for the boiling down, then finish it and bottle it in the cabin," said Patti, nodding her head excitedly.

Mom had her hands over her ears. "Stop! Stop!" she cried.

"Snowshoes," said Jamie, ignoring Mom. "I wonder if I could *make* some? They'd look good hanging on the outside of the cabin ..."

Joan and Patti sat on the cabin step in the afternoon sunshine. They had come with Little Guy after lunch to finish packing up their camp down by the creek, and load the tent and sleeping bags into the wagon. The old tarp was lashed tightly over their stack of camp firewood to keep it dry.

"I'll haul this wood over to the cabin when we get the stove in," Patti had promised.

Then they had carried all of Joan's pots, pans, and dishes in the wheelbarrow, and stacked them carefully in a corner on the cabin floor. Some day, there would be shelves and cupboards to put them in.

Aunt Kate would arrive very soon, in time to have a quick cup of tea with Mom up at the house, then she would come down to admire the cabin. She and Joan would then head back to the city to spend the rest of the day with her brother and sisters, and with Joan's father, who was Aunt Kate's brother. In the morning, Joan would say goodbye to the little ones, and they would begin their long drive back to their father's home in Calgary.

School would start on Tuesday.

"I'll miss the kids, that's for sure," Joan mused. "Not my father, though. I hardly know *him*. But the kids ..."

She sighed. "Mostly, I'll miss being able to talk to them on the phone a couple of times a week. I guess I'll have to start writing letters."

"Do you wish you were going to Calgary with them?" Patti asked.

"Nope." Joan's dark ponytail shook vigorously. "Aunt Kate says my guitar lessons start right away. This week. I wouldn't miss *that* for anything!"

Patti's mind slipped away from the conversation for a moment to consider what life was going to be like on the farm without Joan. Could she even remember now how mixed up she had felt last June when Joan's mother died? This whole summer had been so busy, so full of new things. There had been good times and bad times too, but the cabin had been built; everything on the farm seemed changed in some way she couldn't explain … but it was okay.

"Joan's summer," she said out loud.

"What?" exclaimed Joan, interrupted in the middle of a sentence.

"Oh, sorry," said Patti. "I was just thinking. What were you saying?"

"Aunt Kate is great," Joan explained again. "I like her a lot. When I was little, I used to stay with her practically the whole summer. It's crazy, but I even used to pretend that I really belonged to *her*, and that Mom was just borrowing me for a while." She laughed a little sadly. "Poor

Mom. It's strange, isn't it—how things happen. Maybe after I've lived with Aunt Kate for a while, her place, too, will seem like home to me."

"Well, you're going to spend next summer in Calgary with the kids," Patti reminded her. "Do you think that could ever seem like a *third* home?"

"Who knows?" Joan laughed. "*Three* homes! At the beginning of the summer, I thought I didn't have any home at all! But this is my *real* home for now," she said, echoing Mom. She looked up at the little cabin as it shone in the late summer sunshine. "I wonder if it'll always seem like that."

"Doesn't it bother you at all," Patti asked, "that we ran out of time, and *I'm* going to have the fun of finishing up the inside? Because it bothers *me*."

"No. I don't mind." Joan was positive. "I'm going to be busy too, you know."

"But you *love* projects," Patti protested. "Just as much as I do!"

"It all depends on what you want to *do* with a project, I guess," Joan said. "For me, building a cabin was making a home. That's what I needed: a home. And now I have one."

Patti thought about that. "I see what you mean," she said at last. "That's what building the cabin meant to you. But I always love just doing a project, any project—especially if it's big and complicated and I can get all excited about it … Which reminds me—Mom said last night that we can go through Gramma's boxes in the attic for stuff for the cabin. There are heaps of things there that wouldn't fit in her little place in town, and she says we can have whatever we want. Curtains and tablecloths and knick-knacks. And cushions and scatter rugs. It'll be *so* much fun! But you won't be here to tell me what you like."

"There's always the phone," said Joan. "And I can always toss it all out again when I come back at Thanksgiving." She gave Patti a jab with her elbow. "And don't forget you'll have all the work part of things too— like filling in the cracks between the logs to keep out those winter winds. What are you going to use for that?"

"I don't know yet," Patti admitted. "Of course, it *should* be mud all smunched up with grass. Or cow patties mixed with hay. Yeah—*that* would be the best idea!"

"Yuck," said Joan, obligingly.

"Dad says he'll think about it," Patti said. "He thinks maybe plaster. Or cement. As long as it can be made waterproof on the outside."

"Jamie's just like you, isn't he—when it comes to projects," Joan laughed. "He's been planning furniture like crazy these days. Bunk beds for us. I told him I don't mind the old table from the summer kitchen your Mom offered, but he wants to make one himself. It's easy to see what building the cabin means to *him*."

"Mom's the most amazing one, though, don't you

think?" Patti was still a bit surprised by the changes in her mother. "She isn't going to put any food things in the Fall Fair this year. And this is *Mom* we're talking about— no cookies or cakes or pickles or relish or jams. She's too busy this year finishing up the two carvings she's been working on for the Art display at the Fair. If you ask me, that's the *weirdest* thing that's come from this cabin project. Who would have guessed she was a carver—not just a Mom?"

"What about your dad?" Joan asked. "What do you think the cabin means to him?"

"I think he answered that one today!"

There was a long silence, then, in the sunny warmth of the cabin step—the smell of ripe fields not far away, the distant hum of a tractor, the chirp of a cricket or two.

Patti thought of something. "I'll look after all the things you left behind in the bedroom," she promised. "The pictures and stuff that you brought from your house. Maybe at Thanksgiving you can bring them down here and put them where you want them, once we've got some furniture."

Joan nodded, then cocked her head to listen. Faint voices and laughter drifted down through the woods from the field not far away. Aunt Kate and Mom, coming for the inspection!

"I'll go and pick them up," said Joan, leaping up. "Is Little Guy still hitched up to the wagon?"

Patti nodded, and watched her friend's long-legged run down the path. "Joan's summer," she said once more to the cabin and quiet woods. Because that's what it had been.

"Giddup! Giddup!" came Joan's call from the cleared campsite. The old wagon creaked and rattled, and Little Guy's hooves clip-clopped on the dry path.

Patti grinned. Joan said that *exactly* like Mr. Anderson!

Dad's drawings for Joan and Patti

About the Author

Author photo by Bill Gardam

Heather Gardam was an English teacher originally, and obtained a second B.A. in Creative Writing from the University of Victoria. She has published essays and articles in the *United Church Observer* and *Cruising World*. Her three books, *Life on the Farm*, *Little Guy*, and *Joan's Summer*, originally published by Penguin, were influenced by her experiences as a child on a farm in Ontario, and by her small farm on Salt Spring Island where she and her husband have lived and farmed for thirty-six years. They have three daughters and seven young grandchildren.